SUMMER OF A STRANGER

Carole Gift Page

MOODY PRESS
CHICAGO

*In memory of
Mom and Pop Curren
and Millbrook*

———————

© 1992 by
CAROLE GIFT PAGE

ISBN: 0-8024-8177-9

1 2 3 4 5 6 Printing/LC/Year 96 95 94 93 92

Printed in the United States of America

1

The streamlined Superliner roared into the Springfield Amtrak station with a frenzied flashfire of light and movement—sun glinting off metal, the earth rumbling under the speeding engine's looming shadow.

Kasey Carlone watched with hammering heart as the huge passenger train wheezed to a shuddering stop beside the quaint old depot. *It's truly happening*, she marveled. *I'm really going away, leaving my family behind.*

In a rush of emotion, she whirled around and hugged her mother hard. "Mom, I'm going to miss you so much!"

"Me, too, honey. You take care of yourself, you hear?"

They gazed at each other for a long moment. Her mom's short, coppery brown hair was mussed and her usually impeccable makeup smeared with tears. Kasey knew her own mascara was running too. "It'll only be for the summer, Mom."

"I know. You've got to go. Grandma needs you. We'll be fine."

"All abo-oard!" shouted the conductor, a tall lumberjack of a man in a crisp black uniform.

"Better go, Kasey," said her father, giving her a big bear hug. "Call us from Grandma's."

Her older brother, Keith, gave her a hug too. There was even a hint of wistfulness in his sturdy, chiseled features. Tossing back his thatch of straw-blond hair, he said, "So long, Goggles. Tell the old gang I said hi. And Grams and Gramps too."

Kasey instinctively pushed her glasses up on her nose. "I've told you a million times, Keith, don't call me 'Goggles.'"

"Sorry, Kase. It's just my little term of endearment for you."

"Yeah, sure. Like 'Moose-face' is my pet name for you." She tweaked his cheek. "Keep an eye on Ryan for me, OK?"

"Don't worry. I'll keep the girls so busy they won't have time for Ryan. You go have a blast in Middleton."

"I'm not going for fun, Keith. I'm going to help Grandma Carlone."

"I know, but have a little fun anyway. We—we'll miss you."

Kasey spoke over a growing lump in her throat. "I'll miss you, too. 'Bye, Mom—Dad—Keith. I love you!"

The conductor stepped down and picked up Kasey's carry-on bag as she climbed the steps into the sleek, silvery passenger car. From the open doorway, she looked back and waved good-bye one last time, but she knew if she stood watching her family another moment, she would dissolve in tears. So she grabbed up her bag and gingerly made her way down the long, narrow aisle to a window seat. Already the diesel fumes were giving way to the musky scent of aged upholstery.

Kasey scooted close to the window and looked out toward the train station. She could still see her parents, but they couldn't see her now. They were turning and talking to each other and beckoning to Keith as if they had already forgotten her.

Kasey felt a sudden, wild impulse to jump up and dash off the train back into their arms. She didn't want to be separated from them for an entire summer. Her family had never been apart for more than a few days. How could she endure a whole summer away from them?

Kasey pressed her face close to the window and waved, but still her parents didn't see her. She knocked on the window, knowing it was a useless gesture. Then she watched in frustration as her mother, then her dad, scanned the coach cars, looking for her. The windows were tinted. They would never spot her. She felt an empty space yawning inside her heart. Her parents weren't even out of sight yet, and already she felt painfully cut off from them.

Oh, if only Grandmother Carlone hadn't fallen and broken her hip! If only she didn't need Kasey's help for the summer!

It was strange, mused Kasey. Totally ironic. Less than a year ago her heart had broken when her family moved away from the small farming community of Middleton. They had lived there near her grandparents all of her life. She had hated the idea of moving to Springfield to live—a city ten times the size of Middleton—a place where for many months she felt like a stranger, lost and alone.

And yet now, her heart wrenched at the idea of leaving Springfield. So much had happened this past year, so many experiences Kasey had never anticipated. She had made so many new friends—Selena Hubbard, an overweight girl who fought her own battle against loneliness; Jenny Clegg, a deaf girl who had taught Kasey to listen in a whole new way; and, most important, Ryan Dimarco, the handsome, brown-eyed boy Kasey had grown to love. Leaving Ryan was perhaps hardest of all. *What if he meets another girl over the summer*, she wondered, *someone he cares about as much as he cares about me? What if his heart belongs to someone else when I return home at the end of the summer?*

Kasey's thoughts snapped as the locomotive's whistle sounded and the conductor shouted, "La-ast call! All abo-ard!" The Superliner lurched forward and groaned into motion. For an instant, Kasey's mother spotted her in the window, and they both waved frantically. But just as quickly, her family slipped from her line of vision. Now they were truly gone from her. She would not see them for nearly three months.

Three months isn't so long, she told herself, lifting her chin resolutely and straightening her shoulders. Surely she could get along without her family for one summer.

The noise of grinding gears and heavy wheels straining over worn tracks thundered in Kasey's ears. The train car swayed and bumped and rattled along, already putting distance between Kasey and the Springfield Amtrak station where her parents stood.

Kasey settled back in her seat and swallowed the lump in her throat. It was silly to feel such anguish, as if she were six instead of sixteen. She was nearly an adult. This was only the beginning of being out on her own in the world, making her own way. She had better get prepared; she would not always have her family to depend on. But right now, that knowledge was small comfort. *Face it*, she mused, *I'm a homebody at heart, not a swashbuckling adventurer!*

She laughed inwardly at the bizarre image. Swashbuckling wasn't the proper image at all; that word was reserved for pirates, for Errol Flynn in late-night movies on

TV. She could imagine the gallant hero darting about on some precipice, clashing swords with some dastardly villain or saving some damsel in distress. No, she was no such bold and brave adventurer, although she could identify quite well at the moment with the damsel in distress.

No, I'm not in distress at all, she argued silently. *I'm beginning an adventure of my own. Only God knows what exciting experiences I'll have this summer, what wonderful people I'll meet, what challenges I'll face that will help me grow strong.* "Help me, Lord," she whispered under her breath. "Whatever happens this summer, help me to be the person You want me to be."

2

Now that the train was chugging along at a jaunty pace, Kasey glanced around curiously at the other passengers. A woman and child sat two seats up, an old man with a mop of gray hair sat across from her, and a young couple obviously in love sat behind her.

Kasey enjoyed watching people, privately studying them from the corner of her eye. She liked taking mental notes of the things people said and did. If she could write stories as well as she played the piano, she would put all the things she learned about people into a book.

Human beings did such strange and fascinating things! Like the child two seats up. He was hanging over the seat swinging his arms and making faces at the people around him. They would look away, trying to ignore him, but inevitably his shenanigans drew them back. With his beady eyes and impish face, he reminded Kasey of a funny little chimpanzee she'd seen in the zoo. Yes, the tyke was a cute little monkey making a total nuisance of himself. And his mom just sat there smiling like he was the greatest thing since frozen yogurt.

And the couple behind Kasey—they were fascinating too. Carrying on like honeymooners. Maybe that's what they were. Would anyone actually take a honeymoon on a train? Kasey could imagine people asking them at the wedding, *Where're you lovebirds honeymooning—New York, Paris, Niagara Falls? Nah, we're riding the rails to good ol' Chicago!* It wasn't Kasey's idea of romance. If the couple weren't honeymooners, well, all Kasey knew was that she and Ryan never behaved like that—in public or in private!

Remembering Ryan made Kasey feel lonely again. She thought about the times he had kissed her—so gently and tenderly. She could remember the fragrance of his aftershave and the smoothness of his cheek next to hers. She had never felt like that about any other boy. *Please, dear Lord, don't let Ryan forget me*, she prayed silently.

She glanced over at the old man across from her, who was turning around talking to the man behind him. His hair was gun-metal gray, and his face as lined as a roadmap. His shirt and trousers were wrinkled and dirty, as if he had slept in them more than one night.

He spoke in an Alabama drawl. "So I sez all ah got in this worl' is mah Social Security check, an' it don' stretch more'n two weeks. Now wha's a body to do? Go hungry? Eat outta garbage cans? You tell me!"

Kasey felt a wave of sympathy for the old man. He reminded her of some of her friends at the Shady Oaks old folks' home. Many of them came to the retirement home with nothing more than the clothes on their backs. But they had found a refuge and a family of sorts at Shady Oaks. And Kasey had had a part in making sure their huge old Victorian house would always be there for them. She remembered how, with Ryan's help, she had organized a fund-raiser talent show to raise money to renovate the house, with the Shady Oaks residents the performers and the stars! What a super job they had done, impressing the entire community with their vitality and talent!

Something else. Kasey would miss playing the piano for her elderly friends. Would they all still be there when she returned in the fall? She dreaded the thought, but she couldn't deny the possibility. Chances were, one or more of Shady Oaks' chairs would be empty.

But at least I'll be in Middleton with Grandma and Grandpa Carlone, Kasey reflected. *They need me more than anyone else right now.*

As the railcar swayed rhythmically, Kasey gazed out the window at the landscape skimming by. City buildings, houses, and networks of highways had quickly given way to wide-open stretches of grassland and golden fields, to gleaming silos and apple-red barns. Kasey could almost smell the alfalfa and goldenrod and the freshly plowed earth after a spring rain. Unexpectedly she felt a sense of anticipation as she pictured herself stepping off the train in Middleton.

Why shouldn't she be excited? Middleton had been her home for fifteen years. Her best friends were still there —Diana Morley, her best buddy since kindergarten; Sandy and Joyce, the Marshall twins; the youth group at Middleton Christian Church; and of course, her class at Middleton High.

If Kasey hadn't moved, she would be graduating next June with the Middleton senior class—a scant twenty-five or more seniors compared with the several hundred at Springfield High. It would be good fun to see all of her friends in Middleton again. Perhaps they would call her "city girl" and envy her metropolitan lifestyle. She laughed aloud, then muffled the sound lest anyone think she had a few bats loose in her belfry.

She glanced around self-consciously. *Do the other passengers look at me the same way I look at them?* she wondered. *Do they size me up, analyze me, try to figure out who I am? Or has anyone even noticed I exist? What do they see when they look at me?*

Kasey imagined herself sitting across the aisle scrutinizing herself. She saw herself as not quite pretty, but not quite plain. In certain lighting, her gray-blue eyes and feathery brows were attractive, but their beauty was usually lost behind her glasses, and her rather ordinary features were overwhelmed by her unruly mane of wheat-brown hair.

At least Ryan finds me attractive, she mused. Of course, Ryan was a rare one. He had a way of looking on the inside, not just the outside. He accepted Kasey for herself, just as her parents and grandparents did.

Kasey reached into her purse and pulled out a Hershey bar with almonds. She tore off the wrapper and bit into the cool, solid milk chocolate. Hershey bars had been her favorite candy since she was five and Grandpa Carlone hid them for her in his shirt pocket. Whenever she came to visit, she would hug him and discover a candy bar in his pocket. He always pretended that it was a big deal, her finding the candy bar.

When she was older, Kasey realized it was just a game, and finally, when she became a teenager, she figured Grandpa Carlone would stop the Hershey bar routine. But he didn't, and they always had a laugh as they recalled long-ago days when "little Kasey" searched Grandpa's shirt pocket for her candy bar.

As Kasey thought about Grandpa Carlone, she recalled his urgent telephone call a few weeks earlier telling them about Grandma Carlone's broken hip. Kasey could still hear her grandfather's deep, tremulous voice as he said, "Listen, Kasey, my girl, is there a chance you could

11

come spend the summer in Middleton and help out around the house until your grandmother's on her feet again? I wouldn't ask it of you, but I got all I can handle with the farm. In fact, I even had to hire me a new man to help out with the chores. But there's no way I can handle the housework and meals and looking after your grandma once she comes home from the hospital."

Kasey hadn't even hesitated. "Of course, I'll come, Gramps. As soon as school is out in June."

It wasn't until she had hung up the phone that Kasey began to think about what—and whom—she would be leaving behind. And even now, she argued with herself that it was selfish to dwell on her own wishes when her grandparents needed her. She would trust the Lord to make this summer a special one. And if she was doing what He wanted her to do, then that was all that counted.

But then, why did she have such mixed feelings inside as the train propelled her onward to Middleton? Why did she feel such an ache inside, a longing to be back in Springfield with her parents, her friends—and Ryan?

Kasey gazed out the window. It was nearly dusk. Already the fireflies were flickering like miniature lanterns, lighting the darkness. Kasey sighed. In less than an hour she would be in Middleton. Why did she have this weird, nagging feeling that something terribly important was going to happen to her this summer, something that could change her life forever?

3

As the great Superliner shrieked to a halt beside the Middleton station, Kasey spotted Grandfather Carlone standing on the platform watching for her. He looked older than she remembered, his crown of hair grayer, his portly frame stouter around the middle. But his grin was the same as she stepped off the train minutes later, and his eyes were merrier than ever as he held out his arms to her.

"Kasey, Kasey, my girl, how you've grown up! Where's the little bambino I remember?"

Kasey laughed as she hugged her grandfather. "I'm still plain old me inside."

"Maybe so, but outside you're becoming a very pretty young lady."

Kasey reached instinctively for her glasses and adjusted them on her nose. As she had reflected on the train, she didn't consider herself pretty, what with her unspectacular face framed by an uncontrollable mop of hair the color of cornbread and molasses. But it was nice to know Grandfather Carlone thought she was attractive.

"You always were a wonderful old flatterer." She chuckled as he picked up her carry-on bag and they headed toward the depot.

"Now how would you know that, young lady?" He smiled, opening the door for her.

"Grams says so. She told me you could charm the wings off a butterfly."

Her grandfather laughed heartily. "Your grandma gives me more credit than I deserve, Kasey, my girl." He always called her that—*Kasey, my girl*. It made her feel special.

"Now, where do we pick up that luggage of yours, gal? I brought my pickup truck. You think it'll hold all your treasures?"

"I brought only three suitcases," said Kasey as they made their way to the baggage counter. "Of course, they're stuffed to the gills."

Grandpa Carlone paused with a look of alarm on his face and patted his vest pocket. "Goodness me, but we've forgotten something mighty important, Kasey, my girl."

"What, Gramps? What's wrong?"

"Surely we haven't been apart so long you don't remember . . ." He eyed her shrewdly and winked, still patting his pocket.

Kasey laughed. "Oh, Gramps, I'm too old for that game!"

"Huh! If I'm not too old, you're not too old!"

Kasey reached into her grandfather's shirt pocket and retrieved her Hershey bar. "Thanks, Gramps. They're still my favorite."

After they had collected her luggage, they headed for her grandfather's truck—a little red, stick-shift Chevy. He tossed her suitcases into the back, and they climbed into the cab. Moments later they were on their way, driving down Middleton's familiar Main Street.

Kasey's eyes drank in all the wonderful, nostalgic landmarks—Stanmeyer's Park, the Dairy Queen, Sears, the Kroger store, Lutzer's Fix-It Shop, Susi's Cafe, and —oh, there it was—her father's general store. Of course, it wasn't his anymore. Diana Morley's grandparents owned it now, and the big sign above it read MIDDLETON EMPORIUM. What a dreadful, fancy name for such a dear old, down-to-earth store!

"How could they do it?" she asked her grandfather. "How could they change the name of our store to something so hideous?"

"Times change, things change, names change, Kasey. They call it progress."

"I call it stupidity, " said Kasey. She realized suddenly how much she wanted everything from her past to still be just the way she remembered it. It was all right if the rest of the world marched full speed ahead through the '90s, but not Middleton.

And yet even as she glanced around, she saw changes. There was a video rental shop, a new electronics store, and even a Taco Bell on the corner where Milton Jasper's old Shell station had been. But, for the most part, Middleton looked just as she had left it, and for that she was glad.

"You know, the Morleys own the general store now," said her grandfather as they headed out of town.

"I know, " said Kasey. "They bought it from Dad last year before we moved. It doesn't look the same anymore."

"No, they tried updating the place—making it ready for the twenty-first century, as old Joshua Morley likes to say. He lets his son run the place and make all the decisions."

"Diana's dad," said Kasey. "He must have named it the Middleton Emporium."

"No, I think that was Mrs. Morley's doing. You recall how she likes putting on airs."

Kasey laughed. She and Diana Morley had been best friends for so many years that she was well acquainted with the little idiosyncrasies of Diana's parents. Diana herself often mimicked them and laughed, vowing that she would never have their hangups. "They're so caught up in money and prestige, they should be living in New York City, not Middleton," Diana told Kasey once.

Kasey felt a wave of indignation as she thought about them turning her dear old general store into something suitable for the twenty-first century.

"So how was Keith's graduation?" asked Grandfather Carlone, breaking into her thoughts.

It took Kasey a moment to focus on her brother and his recent graduation from Springfield High. "It was nice," she said. "Mom and Dad were so proud of him. And Keith looked real handsome in his cap and gown, though he didn't think so. He thought he looked like a dork. You know Keith. If it's not a football uniform, forget it."

"Well, you know your grandmother and I would have been there for his graduation if it hadn't been for Grandma's broken hip."

"I know, Gramps. We all missed you. But Keith loved the watch you sent him."

Grandpa Carlone kept his eyes on the road, but there was an unexpected tenderness in his voice. "My grandfather gave me that watch when I graduated from high school, and he told me to keep it and give it to my own grandson someday. So I was following orders—to my great pleasure, I might add. And I hope someday Keith will give that watch to his own grandson."

"Yeah, if he ever gets married," said Kasey skeptically.

"Why? Doesn't he like girls?"

"That's the trouble. He likes too many of them. I don't think he'll ever settle down to one."

"Time will take care of that, Kasey, my girl. And when Keith meets the right one, he'll know it."

Kasey nodded, but she wasn't sure it worked that way or that it was that simple. She wondered if it would be that way for her. She really cared deeply for Ryan. In fact, if she were the gushy type like her best friend, Diana Morley, she would say she was madly in love with Ryan. But she wasn't sure whether it was the real, honest-to-goodness thing or whether her feelings should be chalked up to a typical teenage crush. Whatever it was, it was a powerful feeling. Already she missed Ryan like crazy!

"Well, does the countryside look familiar?" asked Gramps.

Kasey looked around. "Absolutely!"

Even in the near darkness she could see the rolling fields and the lush oak and sycamore trees. And yes, there was the rambling old barn and the winding dirt road that led up to the sprawling, white-frame two-story with its lovely old screened porch. Suddenly Kasey felt as if she had never been away, as if time had stood still and she was back to last summer, before her move to Springfield.

"Oh, I can't wait to see Grams again," she exclaimed, her heartbeat quickening.

"Well, your grandmother can't wait to see you, Kasey, my girl. She's been counting the days till you arrived. You're the best medicine she could have right now."

Grandfather Carlone pulled the truck up beside the old farmhouse, and Kasey was out the door almost before he turned the engine off. She stepped out into the dew-wet grass and gazed around, drinking in the familiar scents. Honeysuckle was heavy in the night air, and the sweet-smelling hollyhocks, and lilacs freshly in bloom.

Kasey's heart filled to overflowing with a sudden delicious joy. How could she have ever left this enchanting, wonderful world? How could she have left her grandparents behind? "Lord Jesus, thank You for bringing me home," she whispered. Then she dashed up the porch steps, calling, "Grandma Carlone, it's me, Kasey! I'm home!"

4

Kasey found Grandmother Carlone in her big four-poster bed in the roomy master bedroom with its warm, colonial-style furniture. She looked frailer than Kasey remembered, and smaller, sitting there in the big bed with its colorful eiderdown quilts.

Kasey ran into her grandmother's arms and hugged her tight. "Grams, I've missed you so much!"

"Dear Kasey, your granddad and I have been counting the days till you arrived."

Kasey sat on the edge of the bed and studied her grandmother's face. It was more lined than before, but still the same round, rosy, smiling face she carried in her memory. "Are you feeling OK?" Kasey asked. "Is there anything I can get for you?"

Grandma Carlone chuckled and patted Kasey's hand. "I'm doing just fine for an old lady who was foolish enough to break her hip."

"Mother said you fell off a ladder—"

"That I did. I was canning cucumbers, apricots, and tomatoes, and I was just fetching some Mason jars off the top shelf—and, well, you can guess the rest."

"I told her she should have asked Dusty to get the jars. That's what we hired him for, to help out around the place."

"Now, Tonio, dear, we hired him to help you on the farm, not me with my baking and canning."

"Then you should have asked me to fetch the jars, Emma."

"You were out in the field with Dusty!"

"Dusty?" Kasey interjected. "Who's Dusty?"

"Dusty Jernigan," said her grandfather. "You'll meet him. Nice boy. Real quiet. Helps out around the farm, and sometimes in the house too, when your grandmother lets him."

"When there's heavy work to do. Of course, with my broken hip, we'll need his help more than ever."

"But that's what I'm here for, Grams."

"I know that, Kasey, but there'll be times when you need a hand around the place, and your granddad and I want you to feel free to call on Dusty."

"Where's he from? I don't recall any Jernigans around Middleton."

"Oh, he's not from around here, " said her grandfather. "He's from somewhere out West. Never did ask where. He just showed up one day looking for work, and I figured I could use a good strong boy like him. Haven't regretted hiring him for a minute. He works hard and minds his own business. A fine lad."

"Where does he live?" asked Kasey.

"He sleeps in the bunkhouse out back. He doesn't seem to mind roughing it. Sometimes he eats his meals with us. Since your grandma got laid up, he's even done some of the cooking."

"And I hate to admit it," said her grandmother, "but he's not half bad if you don't mind plain cooking."

Kasey smiled. "I'm glad you said that, because that's what I cook best too. Plain and simple things like hamburgers and hot dogs and macaroni and cheese."

"Well, Kasey, my girl," said her grandfather, "I'll surprise you sometime with your great-grandmother Carlone's special spaghetti recipe. A body hasn't eaten Italian until he's had her spaghetti."

"I remember, Gramps. It's the greatest."

"But tonight you'll have to settle for warmed-over beef stew."

"That sounds terrific too," said Kasey, "but I can cook something if you like. I want to help out however I can."

"There's plenty of time for that, Kasey. You just rest tonight. Dusty made a big pot of stew yesterday. It'll probably last all week."

"OK, then I'll fix some biscuits to go with it."

"And I'll get your luggage from the truck and put it in your room. You'll be sleeping downstairs, same as us, Kasey. We don't use the upstairs much anymore. Too hard climbing them steps."

"Which room is mine?"

"The pink bedroom with the ruffled curtains and the old rolltop desk you like so well."

"That's my favorite room," Kasey exclaimed.

"I know, gal. It was your dad's room when he was a boy. Of course, it was the *blue* room then." He chuckled. "But you've heard all this before."

"But I love hearing it again!" Kasey turned toward her bedroom, then back again. "Before I get settled in my new room, I'd better go make those biscuits." She looked at her grandmother. "Would you like me to bring you a tray?"

"That would be fine, dear. It'll still be a week or two before I'm up in a wheelchair."

"But just you wait, Kasey," said her grandfather. "When your grandma gets her wheels, there'll be no keeping her down!"

For dinner, Kasey and Grandpa Carlone set up TV trays beside her grandmother's bed so that they could eat together. When they had finished, Kasey washed the dishes and straightened the kitchen, then meandered out to the front porch where her grandfather was sitting.

"Is Grams asleep?" she asked.

He nodded. "Dreaming the dreams of the innocent. Like a baby. She's more at peace since you arrived, Kasey, my girl."

"I'm glad. I hate seeing her confined to bed. She's always been so active, so full of life."

"She'll be her old self in no time. Fact is, you've already lifted her spirits so much, it's a wonder she's not dancing on her toes right now."

"Oh, Gramps, you always know just what to say."

"No, not always, but I'm glad you think so."

Kasey gazed out the screen at the darkened yard. The moon was full, casting silvery ribbons over the treetops and across the grass. It was a beautiful night—a typically warm and muggy June, but the air was bursting with wonderful country smells. Kasey had forgotten how pungent the air was, and how bright the moon shone, and how quiet the earth was on her grandparents' farm. There was no highway roar, no city sounds, no traffic noises. She could hear only the lonely song of crickets and an owl *hoo-hoo-ing* in a distant tree.

"I wish it wasn't so late." She sighed. "I'd love to explore the farm tonight."

"Go have yourself a look, Kasey, my girl. A little look around to tide you over till tomorrow."

She reached over and patted her grandfather's arm. "Thanks, Gramps. I'll just walk down by the barn and come right back."

He laughed lightly. "I'll sit right here waiting."

Kasey was careful not to let the screen door slam. She didn't want to wake her grandmother. She headed down the winding dirt path behind the house, following the streams of milky-white moonlight to the barn. She felt a heady sense of freedom and delight. She could be totally herself here. She could run and chase squirrels or milk a cow or lie on her back in the grass and count the stars. She could pick hickory nuts and wild strawberries and plump, juicy huckleberries. She could be a kid again, and no one would think she was weird.

Kasey reached the barn and stopped. The door was bolted, so she couldn't go in. It was just as well, this time of night. But seeing the old barn brought back a flood of memories—the times she and Keith had played in the hayloft and made secret forts in the straw, the morning the calico kittens were born, the day Gramps's favorite mare took sick and died.

With a shudder, Kasey remembered the mischievous things she and Keith did too. Once they tried to dissect a slippery green frog from the creek down the road, but it got away before they could do any damage. And they caught fireflies in milk bottles and pretended they were lanterns when they hiked in the woods after dark. Worst of all, they caught flies and tossed them into the spider webs behind the barn and watched the spiders spin silky webs around their helpless prey.

Kasey shivered as the night breeze prickled her skin with goose bumps. She didn't like thinking of those flies trapped by ugly black spiders. She didn't like remembering that she could be cruel enough to enjoy watching the macabre dance of a villain devouring his victim. She had learned a lot since her childhood about kindness and compassion. And, no doubt, God had many more lessons to teach her.

But this wasn't the time to think about lessons or spiders or even childhood memories. Kasey had been away from the house too long, and Gramps might get worried. She could explore the farm more freely in the daylight when the world seemed less ominous, when the gnarled old weeping willow no longer cast its eerie shadows across the moonlit barn. She knew she was being silly, but already her imagination was turning the shadow-branches into withered arms reaching out to grab her.

Then, something rustled in the bushes. Something real, something actually there. Not just her imagination!

Kasey turned abruptly, ready to retrace her steps, ready to run, if necessary. Ready to scream for her grandfather.

But the towering shadow of a man blotted out the moonlight as a rough hand seized her arm. A strange male voice demanded, "Who are you, and what are you doing here!"

5

Kasey's mouth went dry and her heart started pounding like a jackhammer. She threw up her hands and uttered, "Please, don't hurt me."

The tall stranger released her arm, still a Goliath-like silhouette against the moon-washed sky. "Who are you?" he barked.

"Kasey," she managed with a little squeak.

The man stepped back. "Kasey?"

"Kasey Carlone," she whispered between shivers of fright.

The man slapped his thigh and laughed. "Well, why didn't you say so in the first place?"

Kasey squinted, trying to make out the man's features. "Do I know you?"

"Naw." He reached out and pumped her hand. "I'm Dusty. Dusty Jernigan. The hired man."

Kasey spoke over the lump in her throat. "You scared me out of my wits with your John Wayne routine."

"I'm sorry, but it's my job to keep an eye on things. For all I knew, you were a cat burglar."

"Right. My grandfather keeps his valuables in the barn, between the baling wire and the horseshoes."

"OK, so I made an honest mistake. It's not the end of the world."

Kasey put her hands on her hips, her terror somersaulting into anger. "Easy for you to say. I thought it was the end of *my* world when you pulled your stick-'em-up routine!"

"Come on. I didn't pull a gun on you. I just figured anyone out here this time of night was up to no good." He put his hands on his hips, matching her stance. "In fact, what were you doing out here in the dark?"

"Taking a walk. Exploring, if it's any of your business."

"Seems like a crazy time to be out exploring. A decent girl belongs inside where it's safe."

"I *am* a decent girl, Mr.—Mr. Jernigan!"

"Call me Dusty. My dad's Mr. Jernigan."

"All right, Dusty. Whoever. Now you've made me forget what I was saying."

"You were saying you're a decent girl."

"Well, I am. For sure. In fact, I'm too decent to be standing here in the middle of the night talking to my grandfather's hired hand. So if you'll excuse me—" Kasey straightened her shoulders and lifted her chin resolutely. "Good night, Mr.—er, Dusty."

He turned and quickly matched her stride. "Would you like me to see you to the porch? You never know what's lurking in the shadows."

"I think I can find my way from here," she said crisply. She marched up the porch steps and opened the screen door.

"Suit yourself." The young man shrugged and turned away. He had taken only a few steps when Kasey's grandfather came to the door and said, "Well, Kasey, my girl, you're back. Oh, and Dusty, come on in. I want you to meet my granddaughter."

Dusty made a sound in his throat, not quite a chuckle. "I think we've already met, sir."

"Well, come on in, my boy, and have a Pepsi or some iced tea. It's a warm evening."

"Thanks," said Dusty, reaching for the screen door. "Don't mind if I do."

Kasey and Dusty followed her grandfather inside and headed for the kitchen. Kasey opened the refrigerator. "We have a big pitcher of sun tea."

Gramps got the glasses. "That sounds good to me."

"Me, too," said Dusty. "With plenty of ice."

Kasey brought the drinks to the table, and they all sat down. For the first time she got a good look at the new hired hand. Dusty had a sturdy, tanned face with a straight nose and solid jaw. But what Kasey noticed most were his eyes. They were a clear, light blue, and they shone with an intensity that made Kasey's stomach turn flipflops. A thatch of golden, wheat-brown hair cascaded over his forehead and curled around his ears. In spite of his rough-hewn appearance and his patched Levi's and torn shirt, he was one of the most handsome men Kasey had ever seen.

"I guess I look pretty grubby to a city girl like you," said Dusty, eyeing her skeptically.

"No, I'm sorry, I didn't mean to stare. I'm not a city girl. I grew up right here in Middleton. You just look like you've had a long day in the fields. You must be a hard worker."

"He is," Kasey's grandfather declared. "The best I've had."

"I got a good boss," Dusty said simply, swallowing the last of his tea. He stood up and gazed down at Kasey. "I'd better head out to the bunkhouse and hit the sack. I hope you enjoy your stay, Miss Carlone."

"Thanks. Call me Kasey, OK?" She walked him to the door. "Good night, Mr.—uh, I mean, *Dusty*."

When she returned to the kitchen, her grandfather was setting the glasses on the counter. "Looks like you and my hired hand might get along OK. Nice looking boy, isn't he?"

Kasey felt her face grow warm. "I hardly noticed, Gramps. Besides, he's too old for me. He must be in his twenties."

"Nineteen. Three years between you. Same difference between your grandma and me."

"Well, if you must know, I—I was just being polite."

Her grandfather laughed. "Well, Kasey, my girl, there's politeness—and there's *politeness*. I saw the way your eyes lit up when you looked at him."

"I already have a boyfriend back in Springfield," Kasey said defensively. "Ryan Dimarco. He's a wonderful guy."

"Humph! I don't see a ring on your finger. Besides, when you're sixteen, that's the time to play the field. Get to know lots of boys. Otherwise, how do you know what kind of fellow you want to marry?"

Kasey threw up her hands in protest. "Gramps, I'm not even thinking about marriage! I still have college, and my career—"

"Your career?"

"You know I want to be a concert pianist."

"And not a wife? A mother? You can't work them in somewhere?"

Kasey shook her head, flustered. "Sure, someday I want to get married, have kids."

Her grandfather ruffled the top of her head. "Some-day comes sooner than you think, child." He lumbered out to the living room. "I'm going to watch the news, Kasey, then head for bed."

She followed him. "Is there anything I can do for Grams before I go to my room?"

"No, I'll see that she's settled in for the night. But we rise early around here, you know, so we'd be grateful for your help with breakfast."

"I'll set my alarm for six, Gramps."

"Sounds good, Kasey. See you in the morning." He kissed her forehead. His eyes were crinkly with warmth and merriment.

Kasey hugged him impulsively. "I love you, Gramps. And I love being back with you and Grams."

"We love you too, Kasey. More than you'll ever know."

Kasey felt a catch in her voice. "I'll just peek in on Grams and see if she's still awake."

"She'll like that."

Grandma Carlone was still awake and reading her big, worn Bible. When Kasey entered the room, she looked up and smiled. "I was just reading the Psalms, Kasey. My favorite book."

"Mine, too." Kasey sat down on the side of the bed. "Can I get you anything, Grams?"

"No, child. It's just so wonderful to have you here. We've missed you and your family since you moved to Springfield. It's been a lonely place around here this past year."

"We've missed you and Gramps too."

"I don't suppose there's any chance of your mom and dad moving back here."

"I don't think so. Dad's really trying to make a go of his new job. And Keith starts Springfield Community College in the fall. And I'll be a senior at Springfield High.

Mom's even started a neighborhood Bible study. So now that we're getting used to Springfield, we like it a lot."

"Well, that's what counts. I want my family to be happy."

Kasey kissed her grandmother good night and walked to the door. "Call me if you need me, Grams."

"I'll be fine. Sleep tight, Kasey." Her grandmother smiled and winked. "And don't let the bedbugs bite."

Kasey laughed and blew a kiss. "I won't, Grams. See you in the morning."

In her cozy little room, Kasey prepared leisurely for bed, slipping into Keith's cast-off Springfield High T-shirt. It was roomy and made a great nightshirt. Besides, it reminded her of home.

She would unpack tomorrow and hang her pictures and set out her treasures to make the room her own. But for now, she reached into her overnight bag and brought out her stuffed Winnie the Pooh, her "companion" since her crib days. He was worn and floppy now, his bright orange color faded to a pale pastel from too many washings. But she loved him anyway.

Kasey sat down cross-legged on the bed and hugged her Pooh bear. She gazed around the quaint old room that had been her dad's when he was a boy. It was hard to imagine her father being little and sleeping in this very room. Did these walls still hold all the words he had ever said? Did he lie in this very bed and stare at the ceiling and dream of the person he would be someday? Did he ever stop to think that someday his daughter would occupy his room and wish she had known him as a little boy?

But the room no longer bore the stamp of a little boy. Grams had made it over with gingham and chintz on the windows, antique portraits on the walls, and colorful rag rugs on the gleaming hardwood floor. Kasey breathed in deeply. The room smelled wonderfully of cedar chests and flower sachets and spicy potpourri. Yes, Kasey could be happy here for a summer.

She pulled back the eiderdown quilt, slipped between the cool white sheets, and fluffed the feather pillow under her head. She tucked Pooh in beside her, then reached up and turned off the little hurricane lamp on the bedstand. As she lay back and gazed up into the darkness, she thought of one of Grams's old sayings: *As snug as a bug in a rug.* Funny, that's just how she felt.

She felt weary, too, but not really sleepy, with an undercurrent of excitement lingering from her train trip. She had mixed feelings—a twinge of yearning for her family back home mingled with joy at being here with her grandparents.

And there was something else. Surprising. Disconcerting. She couldn't get out of her mind the image of a tall, rugged, brooding young man. Her grandfather's hired hand. Dusty Jernigan.

6

The next day, after Kasey had completed her chores and spent an hour practicing the piano, she telephoned her friend Diana Morley.

"Yes, it's really me," she exclaimed. "Didn't my grandparents tell you I was coming?"

"Well, the truth is," said Diana, "I don't see much of your grandparents anymore."

"But you must see them at church every Sunday, although I suppose with Grams's broken hip, they've missed the past few weeks."

"So have I," said Diana. "The past few months, in fact."

"How come? Have you been sick?"

"No, nothing like that. I've just been busy working at the Emporium—that's the new name for the store—"

"Yeah, I noticed. You mean it's open on Sundays now?"

"Well, my dad figured we were losing a lot of business being closed on Sundays, and he was right. We're doing a lot better being open seven days."

"So you're working a lot of hours then?"

"Yeah. I need the cash. And what else is there to do in Middleton? You know how dead it can be around here, especially in the summer. You were lucky to get out when you did."

"I don't know," said Kasey. "I've missed the town a lot, and the people—like you and Sandy and Joyce. I've even missed working in the store."

"Well, we can solve that easily enough. Come back to work for the summer."

"Oh, I'd love to, but I came back to Middleton to help Grams around the house."

"So get your work done there, then spend a couple hours a day at the store. You'll need some spending money, won't you?"

"True. And I bet Grams wouldn't mind, as long as I planned my schedule carefully."

"Terrific. I'll talk to my dad about it. I know he'll be glad to have you back. You know the store almost better than anyone."

"When can we get together?" asked Kasey. "I can't wait to catch up on old times."

"How about now? I don't have to be at the store until four."

"Great. Shall we meet at our favorite old haunt?"

"The Dairy Queen? Sounds like a plan. Want me to pick you up?"

"Pick me up?" echoed Kasey. "Are you saying—no! —have you got your own car?"

"Only the best wheels in town. A red Mustang convertible. Daddy bought it for my sixteenth birthday. I just pay for gas and insurance."

"A convertible? I can't believe it! Come get me. I can't wait to take a ride!"

Diana arrived before Kasey even had a chance to run a brush through her hair or put on blush and lip gloss. As Kasey rushed to the door, she wondered if Diana would think she had changed. Would they still feel like best friends?

Kasey opened the door and did a double-take. "Diana? Is that really you? You look like you just stepped out of *Vogue* magazine!"

Diana sashayed inside like a model showing off the latest Parisian fashions. She was wearing an embroidered vest, silk, plum-colored shirt, and capri leggings. Her flowing blonde tresses were several shades lighter than Kasey remembered. "You like it, Kasey? It's my new look. I had to go all the way to Bloomington for these clothes. Wait'll you see. It's the only place to shop."

"You—you have to dress like that to work at the store —uh, Emporium?"

"No, of course not. I do this for me. I'm making a statement. Do you like?"

Kasey shrugged. "I'm not sure. What's the statement?"

Diana frowned. "Really, Kasey, don't be obtuse. You've lived in Springfield nearly a year. Surely living in a big city has made you more sophisticated."

Kasey felt her confidence quickly deflating. "I don't know if I'm more sophisticated or not. I haven't thought much about it."

Diana sat down on the sofa and crossed her legs with obvious finesse. "Well, I think you've improved since last year. You look older, almost pretty. If you'd just throw away those glasses and get contact lenses. Listen, I can do your colors if you like and show you some great makeup techniques."

"Sure. I'd like that," said Kasey half-heartedly. In all her months of missing her best friend, Kasey had forgotten how brittle and aggressive Diana could be—and how self-centered. Or had those traits simply grown more pronounced with time?

"Are you listening, Kasey?" Diana chided. "I said, you'll have to go with me to Bloomington sometime. For the weekend."

"A whole weekend? Where would we stay?"

"With my friend Sonja Taggart. She's already in college. And, would you believe, she has her own apartment!"

"Well, I couldn't get away for a whole weekend, not with Grams laid up—"

"OK, overnight then. Promise. We'll have a blast."

"We'll see." Kasey reached for her purse. "Are we ready for the Dairy Queen?"

Diana squeezed Kasey's arms excitedly. "Are you ready for the ride of your life?"

Diana drove her gorgeous new convertible too fast, as Kasey knew she would, but the wind whistling through Kasey's hair perked up her spirits and reminded her how much fun Diana could be. From their earliest years they had set out on adventures together, determined to conquer the world. Diana had always made Kasey feel that anything was possible, even in a one-horse town like Middleton. Diana was fond of saying, "They may roll up the sidewalks at dusk, Kasey, but they can't put out the fire in our spirits. Someday we'll show them what we can do!"

Kasey had done just that with her music, playing the piano at church every Sunday to the delight and applause of the townspeople. But Diana was still looking for her place in the sun; at least she was still looking last summer when Kasey moved away. Now, it looked as if Diana had found her niche—in Bloomington.

Diana pulled up beside the Dairy Queen and parked. She fished in her purse for a Kleenex and blew her nose.

Kasey wiped tears from her eyes and laughed. "Some wind, huh? Got us both blubbering."

"No, it's my allergies. They act up in the summer."

"I didn't know you had allergies."

Diana gave her an odd glance. "I always have, Kasey. You just forgot."

They went inside and ordered large cones with chocolate coating, then sat at an outside table under a maple tree devouring their creamy desserts before they melted. "Do you still come here a dozen times a week?" asked Kasey.

Diana shook her head. "Hardly ever."

"What? You—the ice cream fiend of Middleton?"

"I've lost my taste for it, Kasey. We all have to grow up sometime, you know."

"Well, when I've lost my taste for ice cream, I'll know I'm too old."

"There are other things in life, some things even better than ice cream."

"Like what?"

"Come with me to Bloomington some weekend and find out."

"You sound awfully mysterious."

"I'm not trying to. I just think you'll be surprised what a good time you can have there."

"I've always had a good time around here, Diana. In fact, I'm having a great time right now."

Diana laughed. "This is kid stuff, Kasey. We're adults now. Almost seventeen. There's a whole wide world out there waiting for us. I figured you would have discovered that by now in Springfield." She licked her ice cream carefully around the edge of the cone. "Tell me what it's like in

Springfield. What are the boys like? What are the girls like? What does everybody do?"

Kasey pressed her lips against the cold ice cream and savored its icy smoothness. She wondered what to tell Diana. Nothing that had happened to Kasey in Springfield would make headlines as far as Diana was concerned. Except maybe Ryan. So, fighting an unexpected self-consciousness, she told Diana about her growing friendship with Ryan Dimarco.

Diana nodded eagerly. "OK, so how close are you? I mean, are we talking fireworks and the Fourth of July?"

"We—we've kissed, if that's what you mean."

"Are we talking serious business, or what?"

"Nothing has happened, if that's what you're implying. Ryan's cool. He's never pressured me for anything that made me feel uncomfortable."

Diana looked disappointed, but she just said, "Oh, that's nice. He sounds very—sweet."

Kasey decided to change the subject. "Tell me what's happened to everyone since I moved away. What's happening at Middleton High? What's new with the church youth group?"

Diana looked a bit bored as she rattled off the whereabouts of the young people they both knew. "Jennifer Gould moved to California, Wendy Platt went away to college—some private school somewhere. I can never remember the name. Sandy and Joyce are still around, when they're not on vacation with their folks, but I don't see them much. Like I said, I don't get to church these days."

"Not at all?"

Diana frowned. "You make it sound like some sort of crime. To tell you the truth, Kasey, church bores me. It's always the same old thing, and I mean, the guys there are all geeks. I'd gag if they asked me out." She licked ice cream from her fingertips. "I've outgrown it, Kasey. Sun-

37

day school was fine when we were little kids, but I'm ready for the real world now."

Kasey eyed her quizzically. "You're ready for the real world? What's the *real world?*"

Diana smiled coyly. "Come with me to Bloomington, and I'll show you."

As Diana headed her sleek convertible back to the farm, Kasey sat quietly mulling over the last hour. She felt a sick sensation in the pit of her stomach that had nothing to do with eating too much ice cream. She wondered, *Is this the girl who was my best friend since kindergarten? Who changed—she or I? Or both of us? And is it too late to get back the closeness we once shared? Do I even want it back?*

"Well, here we are, Kasey," said Diana. "Home again. Give me a call, and I'll let you know what my dad says about you working at the Emporium."

Kasey opened the car door and stepped out. "OK. Thanks."

Diana put her car in reverse, then stopped and gestured toward Kasey. "Hey, who's that man going into your grandparents' house?"

Kasey glanced toward the screened porch. "Oh, that's Dusty, my grandfather's new hired hand."

A smile played on Diana's lips. "New hired hand, huh? Where's he from? What do you know about him?"

"Nothing. Even Gramps doesn't know where he's from. He's sort of a mystery man. But Gramps swears by him."

"That's what this town needs," mused Diana. "Some new blood. He's a real hunk. You'll have to introduce me sometime."

"Sure—sometime," said Kasey uncertainly. She turned and ran toward the house, strangely relieved to be back. One thing she was sure of. Diana Morley and Dusty Jernigan would never make a winning combination!

7

On Sunday morning Dusty drove Kasey to church in the pickup while Grandpa Carlone stayed home with Grams. "I could have driven myself," Kasey told Dusty, "but I don't know how to drive a stick shift, and trucks make me a little nervous anyway. They take up so much of the road."

"No problem," said Dusty. "If your grandfather gives me the time, I can drive you anywhere you need to go."

"Thanks. I sure appreciate it."

Kasey studied Dusty's profile as he sat in the driver's seat, his gaze focused on the two-lane road that would take them from the farm to Middleton Christian Church. Dusty was very good looking—tanned, athletic, with features that were rugged and yet as classic as Greek sculpture. He reminded Kasey of Michaelangelo's famous *David* that she had studied in art class. Only Dusty was no statue; he was very much a real flesh and blood man, with the earthiness of the farm on his hands and sweat on his brow. Kasey found the outdoor smells surprisingly appealing.

Sitting beside him now in the cab of the truck, she felt his energy, his presence, a restless sense of excitement in the air. It was as if he were somehow bigger than life. The feeling was unsettling.

"You know, if you'd like, you could come to church with me," she ventured. "I'm sure Gramps wouldn't mind you taking some time for yourself."

"Thanks, Kasey, but I've got some errands to run. But I'll pick you up at noon sharp."

"OK. Maybe another time."

After church, the pickup was parked beside the curb just as Dusty had promised. Kasey climbed in and smoothed out her sundress.

"So, how was it?" he asked.

"Fine. It was great to see everyone again."

He eyed her curiously. "Really? Then how come you don't look happy?"

"What makes you say that?"

"Your eyes. I see disappointment in them."

Kasey averted her gaze out the window. She didn't want to get into this with Dusty, who was practically a stranger and didn't even consider it important to go to church.

"That's OK," he said as he pulled out onto the street.

"What's OK?"

"You don't have to tell me anything. I'm just the hired hand."

"It's not that," Kasey said quickly. "It's just—it's just that I had such high expectations."

Dusty chuckled. "Yeah, I know how that goes."

Suddenly the words came pouring out. "I thought when I came back everyone would be as excited to see me

40

as I was to see them. I thought it would be so special, with everyone welcoming me home."

"But they didn't, huh?"

"It was totally weird. In a way, it was like any other Sunday. It was almost like I'd never been gone. Some people said hi like they hadn't even noticed I'd been away a year."

"You're kidding!"

"No, but they weren't trying to be unkind. They're just busy with other things. They were friendly and polite, but—"

"But it wasn't the same, huh?"

"No. For me, everything was different. I used to play the piano in church every Sunday, but now they have someone else. They don't need me anymore. And some of my best friends are gone—off on vacation or away at school or working summer jobs out of town. I felt—I don't know—left behind. Everybody's gone on with their lives. I felt like I didn't belong anymore."

"People lead busy lives, Kasey. What's important to us isn't necessarily important to them. The point is, you don't want to let it matter what people say and do. Then they can't hurt you."

Kasey looked over in surprise. "Is that how you feel, Dusty? You won't let yourself care about people?"

"That basically sums it up."

"That's an awful way to feel," she blurted. "If you won't risk being hurt, how can you ever know what love's all about?"

He shrugged. "I don't want to know. I like keeping things simple and uncomplicated. That's the way I live."

Kasey didn't reply. She realized suddenly that the conversation had taken too serious a tone, and she was venturing into topics that were none of her business. She certainly didn't want Gramps's hired man thinking she was nosing around in his affairs.

Kasey spent Sunday afternoon in the kitchen poring over her grandmother's cookbooks. She was determined to put on a spread that would please her grandparents, and, besides, it was time she practiced her culinary skills. In fact, she had used them so seldom she wasn't sure she had any.

She put a chicken in the oven to bake and fixed white rice and broccoli, then set up TV trays by her grandmother's bed. To Kasey's delight, her grandparents raved about the food and assured Kasey she was bound to be another Julia Child.

Later that evening, when Dusty came by after finishing his chores, Kasey offered to put a plate of leftovers in the microwave for him. He looked genuinely pleased. She sat at the table and sipped a Pepsi while he quickly polished off the chicken and rice.

Afterward, he said, "That's the best meal I've had all summer. You're quite a cook, Kasey Carlone."

Kasey beamed. "You're welcome to eat with us anytime you want, you know. Gramps said he told you so when he hired you."

Dusty forked up his last bite of chicken. "I know, but I don't like imposing on folks. I'm not a three-meals-a-day guy anyway. I eat on the run, sometimes just once a day."

"That's not healthy," protested Kasey. "Didn't your mom ever tell you it's important to eat three balanced meals a day?"

Dusty tapped his fork on the china plate and scowled, working his mouth into a sneer that startled Kasey. "My mom was too falling down drunk to know what I ate—or to care."

Kasey nearly choked on her Pepsi. "I—I'm sorry. I didn't mean to stir up bad memories."

Dusty pushed back his chair and stood up. "No sweat. It doesn't bother me anymore. Nothing does. It's cool, OK? Thanks again for the chow. You did good."

Kasey walked him to the door. "Breakfast will be at seven sharp, if you're interested."

He grinned and nudged her under the chin. "Thanks, kid. You're OK."

After Dusty left for the bunkhouse, Kasey slipped out onto the screened porch and rocked in the creaky old swing. The night breeze felt refreshing after a long, hot day, and the quietness gave Kasey some time alone to think.

Since coming back to Middleton, her emotions had been on a roller-coaster ride. She missed everyone back home—her family, her friends, and, of course, Ryan. And yet she was so filled with anticipation over seeing all the people from her past. Now she had seen them—many of them, at least—and she felt like a balloon that had been suddenly deflated. Nothing was the way she had expected it to be. Everyone was kind enough, but it struck her afresh that she wasn't a pivotal part of their lives anymore. The space she had occupied in their hearts had been filled with other things or other people. She could just as easily return to Springfield and it would make no difference to them.

Only Diana Morley seemed eager to resume their friendship, and Diana wasn't even part of the church anymore. What's more, Diana had changed so much from the girl Kasey remembered. Did they still have anything in common?

And then there was Dusty Jernigan, a strange young man who somehow attracted and repelled Kasey at once.

She felt drawn to him, mesmerized by his presence, and yet intimidated by him at the same time. She had never felt such strange vibes from any other person. He stirred some deep emotion that both scared and fascinated her. She sensed that she should keep her distance from him. But that would be very hard to do when they faced an entire summer together on her grandparents' farm.

"Lord Jesus," Kasey said aloud, "You helped me last year when I felt so terrible about moving away from Middleton. Now I'm back and feeling more confused than ever. I thought it would be so wonderful being with all the people I grew up with, but everything's different. The Middleton I remember is nothing like this one, and it makes me feel so sad."

Kasey put her head back on the swing and gazed at the stars. She could see the Big Dipper. It looked brighter here than it did in Springfield. And the crickets were louder, and the flowers smelled sweeter. Then why did she feel so empty inside, so restless, like something was missing?

Kasey fixed her gaze on the sky and thought about Jesus being the God of the heavens and the God of her heart. He was as much with her now as He was in Springfield. He had taught her a lot this past year. Maybe He had more to teach her this summer. Maybe people didn't go on vacation from learning important things about themselves.

She whispered aloud, "Lord Jesus, I know I need to be here to help Grams and Gramps, but this will be my seventeenth summer, and I want it to be special. Please, let it be the kind of summer I always dreamed of." Almost reluctantly, she added, "And if there's stuff You need to teach me, help me to learn so You'll be proud of me."

8

On Monday morning, after Kasey had finished her piano practice and her work for Grams, she went out to the barn and scrounged around for the old bike she had discarded before her move to Springfield. She found it stored with some of her grandfather's tools. It really wasn't in bad shape—maybe just a little rustier than she remembered. And, you might know, the tires were flat.

Just as she was debating how to repair them, Dusty appeared and assured her he could have them fixed in no time at all. True to his word, he had the bike ready for Kasey by lunchtime.

"Where you going?" he asked as she gave the bike a test run around the yard.

"To town. To see about working at the general st—uh, I mean, the Emporium."

"It's a long ride. I could drive you."

"No, that's OK. I've got to do this on my own."

"Suit yourself," he said and turned away. Kasey had a feeling he felt rebuffed, but she didn't have time now to soothe over hurt feelings. Especially when they weren't even warranted.

She pedaled the long, winding road into town, and halfway there she wished she had taken Dusty up on his offer. It was easier going to the store when she lived with her folks just a few blocks from town. But at least a few bike rides like this and she'd be in top form.

Twenty minutes later, Kasey entered the store and looked around expectantly, hoping Diana would be working. She hated facing Diana's parents by herself; they weren't exactly her kind of people. In fact, as far as she could tell, they weren't anybody's kind of people. They were the types you expected to see on TV's "The Rich and the Famous"—only they weren't that rich and certainly not famous.

Moments after Kasey entered the Emporium, she sensed it had been a mistake. In no way was it the general store she remembered. The walls had been painted neon pink and green, and the oak counters and display tables had given way to plastic and Plexiglas. The pharmacy had been replaced by a video rental section, and the farm supplies area was now a fashion boutique.

As Kasey looked around, Mrs. Morley wafted over to her with a benevolent smile. "Well, little Kasey Carlone! Diana said you were back. She tells me you'd like to work here part-time."

"Yes, if you could use me. I have to help out at the farm and keep up with my piano practice, but I could work here a couple hours a day."

"That would be splendid, dear. The customers never stop asking about you. You'll be good for business. Of course, we can only pay minimum wage. I hope that's not a problem."

"No, I can use some spending money."

"Yes, that's what Diana always says," clucked Mrs. Morley. "And can that girl spend!"

Kasey laughed, knowing Mrs. Morley had meant it as a joke. But it was the truth. Diana had always been an avid spender, even in her more conservative days.

"Well," Mrs. Morley was saying, "why don't we fill out the necessary paperwork, and you can start tomorrow."

Afterward Kasey walked around town, meandering in and out of shops, browsing here and there, greeting townspeople she hadn't seen in nearly a year. Everyone was cordial, but it still wasn't like the days when her family owned the main store in town and she knew every customer on a first-name basis. Often, she knew what people had come in for before they even said a word. There was a special camaraderie then that was missing now. She was an out-of-towner now, just visiting. But maybe working at the store again would rebuild some of those old bridges between her and the community. Suddenly, that seemed like her most important goal.

It was nearly dusk when Kasey pedaled up the rutted driveway to the farmhouse, her chest heaving with exhaustion. She was certainly not the sturdy farm girl she had been last summer. Life was too easy in Springfield. She wasn't used to the exertion of working long hours with her hands or even riding a couple miles on a bicycle in the summer heat. Face it, she was soft!

As she wheeled her bicycle into the barn, she spotted Dusty coming up the path from the field. He was carrying a basket of fresh green beans.

"Hey, Kasey, I figured you might like some of these for supper."

"Thanks. They look great. Are you joining us?"

"I don't know. Are you fixing those beans with bacon and onions?"

"I guess I could—if you show me how."

"Be glad to. Soon as I get washed up, OK?"

"OK."

Kasey took the basket and headed for the house. Gramps was in his favorite chair in the living room watching the news on TV. Grams was propped up in bed, doing some mending. Kasey greeted them both, promised to have dinner ready in an hour, then headed for her bedroom to change into her grubbies. As soon as she entered the room, she spotted a letter on her bureau. She recognized the handwriting. It was from Ryan.

Her fingers were already trembling as she tore open the envelope. She sat down on her bed and read Ryan's words with an urgency that surprised her:

Dear Kasey:

You haven't even been gone a week, and already I miss you more than I can say. The summer isn't any fun without you here. I keep reaching for the telephone to call you, and then I remember it's long distance. But I will call you soon, maybe on the weekend. I don't care what it costs.

In fact, I'd drive the 400 miles to see you, but I'm working five days a week and teaching third-grade boys on Sunday, not to mention my regular visits to Shady Oaks. So you can see how impossible it is to get away.

But I want you to know I'm not seeing any other girls. Of course, when would I have time! That doesn't mean you can't see other guys, but I hope you won't. I hope you have room in your heart, and in your dreams, only for me.

There's nothing new here. Life comes to a halt in the summer. Is it that way in Middleton, or are you having a great time seeing all your old friends?

Well, don't forget me. I think of you all the time. Write soon.

Love,
Ryan

Kasey pressed the letter to her heart and fought back tears. "Oh, Ryan, I miss you so much," she whispered. "It feels like you're a million miles away, not just four hundred!"

Carefully she tucked the letter in her top bureau drawer, changed her clothes, and hurried to the kitchen to prepare dinner. She stuck potatoes in the oven to bake, made ground sirloin into patties, then put the green beans in a bowl and sat on the screened porch, snapping off the ends. When she was nearly finished, Dusty arrived, fresh-shaven and smelling of cologne.

"You look nice," she told him as he sat down beside her.

"Thanks. I did it for you."

"For me?" she stammered. "You didn't have to get dressed up for me."

He chuckled. "Well, I never felt inspired to spruce up for your grandfolks, nice as they are, but for a pretty girl—that's another story."

Kasey felt her face grow warm. She wished now that she hadn't changed into her old grubbies. Did Dusty really think she was pretty, or was he just being kind—or worse, was he simply a smooth talker who spouted his line to any available girl?

"I'd better get these beans on," she said, standing up.

He followed her inside. "I'm doing the beans, remember?"

"Oh, right. I'll get the onions and bacon."

Kasey had to admit they made a pretty good team in the kitchen. Dusty knew his way around the stove better than she did, and he fried the ground sirloin to perfection in the same pan he'd fried the onions and bacon—and they were scrumptious!

Kasey's grandfather had his dinner in the bedroom with Grams, while Dusty and Kasey ate at the kitchen table. After dinner Dusty helped her clean the kitchen while Gramps got Grams ready for bed.

"The doctors say Grams can try a wheelchair next week," she told Dusty as they dried the dishes. "She'll be so glad to wheel out to the kitchen table for her meals."

"She's lucky to have you here to help," said Dusty. "You brighten this old place up—for all of us."

Kasey didn't know how to respond, so she ignored the compliment. Instead, she asked, "Have you had a chance to meet many people since you came to Middleton?"

"Naw." He cast her a sidelong glance. "To tell you the truth, I don't have much use for most people. I get into town once in a while for supplies, that's all."

"It must be hard," she ventured, "not having any friends—I mean, close by."

"I'm used to it. I don't have friends anywhere."

"Not even back home? Wherever home is?"

"Nope. My folks traveled around a lot. I never stayed in one place long enough to make friends."

"I'm sorry," said Kasey. "It must have been hard for you."

"Not really. I didn't know any other way."

"Well, I'm sure Gramps would give you time off if you wanted to, you know, make friends here in Middleton."

He grinned at her. "I'm doing OK. But just so you'll feel better—you wanna be my friend?"

Kasey smiled and rolled her eyes. "I think I walked into that."

"Yep."

9

The following Friday, Kasey agreed to go with Diana Morley to Bloomington for the weekend. Grams assured Kasey that she and Gramps could get along without her for a couple days, and, after all, they wanted her to have a little fun this summer, not just spend the whole time playing nursemaid. And since Diana and Kasey had been best friends practically all their lives, it was only natural for Kasey to want to get away and try her wings a little. That was Grams's way of expressing it.

To Kasey, it made her sound like she was an angel or something. *Trying her wings.*

Kasey wasn't really sure what Diana even had in mind with this weekend in Bloomington. What could they do there that they couldn't do with the old gang in Middleton? Diana wanted Kasey to meet Sonja Taggart and her other new friends—girls who were students there at the university and who had their own apartment.

"It's so fab!" Diana had said. "Totally awesome. Wait'll you see it. It must cost them a thou a month. But there's three of them. They split the rent. We could do something like that too, Kasey. When we're both out of high school. We could move to Bloomington and get a place together."

Kasey didn't bother telling Diana that she dreamed of going to Juilliard and studying piano; more than anything in the world, she wanted to be a concert pianist. Well, actually, that was her old wish. She had learned this past year to leave her fondest wishes in God's hands. He knew best. And unless Kasey figured out a way to get the money for Juilliard, she'd probably end up at Springfield Community College, like Keith. But no sense in going into all that with Diana. Kasey had the feeling she wasn't the least bit interested.

In fact, as Kasey and Diana sped along the highway in the red convertible heading toward Bloomington that Friday night, all Diana could talk about was her friend Sonja and Sonja's glamorous apartment.

"It is so posh, Kasey, it makes anything in Middleton look like Tobacco Road. Wait'll you see. You'll never want to go back to ugly tract houses or rundown farms."

Kasey felt a wave of indignation that Diana could dismiss their homes in such disparaging terms, but she kept her feelings to herself. She wanted to gain back the closeness she and Diana had shared in the past, so she was determined to summon some enthusiasm for this weekend venture.

It was nearly eight when they pulled into the parking lot behind the Polynesian Winds apartment complex. It struck Kasey as absurd that an apartment building in the middle of America's heartland should have such an exotic name, but maybe it brought in tenants who wished they were planted in some romantic port instead of a town only a day's drive from the Windy City itself.

Kasey followed Diana up the outside stairs to a second-story apartment. A redhead in a green tunic top and spandex leggings opened the door. "Di, you made it!" she gushed. "Come in. Everyone's here."

Diana urged Kasey into the doorway. "Sonja, this is my friend Kassandra Carlone. She plays a great piano. Kasey, Sonja Taggart."

Sonja was all smiles. "Kassandra—what a dynamite name. So you play a great piano? Fab! All I play is a great radio. Come on in."

"You can call me Kasey," Kasey murmured, but Sonja was already leading them through the ceramic tile entryway to the living room. The decor was contemporary black on white—black sectional sofas and recliners with white carpet and drapes, and glass cocktail tables. It was as cold as winter itself.

Kasey realized that a party was in progress. Bon Jovi was playing on the stereo, and people were milling about chatting and laughing. Somehow Kasey hadn't expected a party. She thought it would just be Diana and herself and Sonja and her roommates.

"Hey, everybody, listen up," said Sonja above the din. "Di's here, and her friend Kassandra. They came a long way. Make them feel at home." She turned back to Kasey. "Help yourself to drinks and those pizza things."

Kasey looked over at the bar just off the dining room. She'd never been in a house with a wet bar. She followed Diana over and helped herself to a pizza roll.

"What would you girls like?" asked a tall blond man with a stubbly beard. "Wine cooler, or something more exotic?"

"Soft drink," said Kasey quickly.

"Wine cooler," said Diana.

Kasey cast her friend a quick glance. Since when was Diana drinking alcoholic drinks?

As if reading Kasey's unspoken question, Diana said, "Don't be a prude, Kasey. Wine coolers aren't really so bad, you know."

Kasey knew better, but she figured this wasn't the time to get into a debate on the subject. She followed Diana over to a group of girls. They all knew Diana and greeted her warmly. One girl with crimped hair and jangly earrings that dangled to her shoulders asked Kasey, "Did Sonja say your name was Capone?"

"No. *Carlone*." Kasey spelled it slowly, enunciating above the heavy rock music beat.

The girl watched her raptly, then inquired, "Are you from one of those Mafia families?"

"No way," Kasey declared, swallowing her indignation.

"Too bad," said the girl. "I thought you might have some great stories to tell."

Another girl asked Kasey, "What's your sign? I'm Libra, although I came this close to being born a Scorpio—"

"I really don't pay any attention to those—" Kasey began, but another girl in a miniskirt cut her off.

"Play something for us, Kassandra," she urged. "Do you play jazz? Or I bet you're into soul. Or—don't tell me —soft rock!"

"Mainly classical—"

An attractive brunette in an embroidered bolero jacket sauntered over with a strapping football-type jock. They helped themselves to drinks, then greeted Diana with hugs and laughter. Kasey endured more introductions, but already she was wishing she had never come. What did she have in common with Diana's friends? In fact, a more burning question, what did she have in common with Diana herself?

"So, Diana says you're going to play for us, Kassandra," said the jock. He wore a flattop, and his neck was so large his head seemed to merge directly with his shoulders.

"I don't think so," Kasey said softly, stepping back as if to make her escape.

"Oh, come on, Kase—uh, Kassandra," Diana urged. "Show them what you can do."

Before she knew it, Kasey was swept over to the black upright piano in the family room. She sat down and drew in a breath, trying to compose herself. Someone had turned off the hard rock, and everyone was suddenly quiet, waiting for her to perform. It would have to be something Kasey knew from memory.

She thought a moment, then, with a sweeping flourish of her fingers over the keyboard, she began to play "Chariots of Fire." The music filled the room with a lilting, triumphant ring, and when she had finished, the walls reverberated with applause.

"Fantastic! Bravo! Encore!" Everyone wanted more.

She played part of a Beethoven concerto, then several hymns, including "Amazing Grace." When she had finished, she sensed the atmosphere in the room had changed. One girl said, "I used to hear that song in church. It's so sad. It makes me cry."

"But it's not sad," Kasey protested. "It speaks of God's love for us, and that's something wonderful—"

"Really, Kasey," whispered Diana, "this isn't church."

"Maybe not, but she plays like the angels, " said Sonja. "I wish I had that kind of talent."

"Aw, come on, Sonja, you can't even play your VCR without messing up," teased the jock.

"I can too. Just wait!" Sonja held her glass high, and declared, "Come on, everybody, back to the food and drinks —especially the drinks! Is this a party, or what!"

As everyone filtered back to the wet bar, the girl in the bolero jacket touched Kasey's arm. "You're a beautiful person. Did anyone ever tell you that? Beautiful inside."

"It's not me, " Kasey said quickly, but how could she explain to this girl that it was the Lord inside her who was beautiful? She groped for words, but the girl had already moved on.

The party went on with a blast of hard rock and a blur of commotion. A few couples danced to Madonna and Prince; others drifted off to the family room and put an R-rated video on the VCR.

Kasey wandered around, nursing a warm Coke, wishing she was back in Springfield with Ryan or at her grandparents' farm swinging on the screened porch. How was she going to endure an entire weekend with Sonja and her friends? Or was she being a prude, as Diana said? Or worse, a snob? She wished she knew what the Lord wanted her to do. *He probably would have said don't go in the first place,* she mused, *but it's too late. I'm already here.*

Later, as Kasey approached the bathroom, she heard Diana and Sonja talking heatedly behind the door. Diana sounded upset. "What do you mean, it'll cost more?" she demanded. "It costs more every time. What kind of scam is this?"

Sonja said, "It's not me. I don't have anything to do with it. They tell me, and I tell you. What else can I say?"

"Tell them they know what they can do with their—"

Kasey retreated quickly back down the hall. Her heart was pounding. She felt as if she had overheard something that wasn't meant for her ears, but what did it mean? Was Diana in some kind of trouble?

Kasey's mind buzzed with questions, but when Diana and Sonja returned to the party, they were laughing and chatting as if nothing was wrong. *Perhaps I misunderstood,* thought Kasey. *Maybe it's nothing at all.*

But the alarm bell had already sounded. More was going on in Diana's life than she wanted anyone to know.

10

Kasey persuaded Diana to drive back to Middleton on Saturday rather than staying over until Sunday. The two girls were quiet most of the way home, until Kasey broke the silence.

"I didn't mean to spoil your weekend, Diana. It's just that I didn't feel comfortable there in Bloomington. I felt it was time to get back home."

"What you mean is, you didn't like my friends," countered Diana coolly as she accelerated the engine.

"It's not that. I just don't think we have anything in common with them."

"Maybe you don't. I do."

Kasey sighed. "You've known me all my life, Diana. You had to know I wouldn't like that kind of party. Why did you invite me?"

"Because I thought after living in Springfield, you'd be ready to expand your horizons like I've done. The real world isn't Middleton, Kasey. It's time you realized it."

"OK, Diana. You tell me. What is the real world?"

Diana didn't respond immediately. Finally she looked over, her blue eyes flashing, and said, "The real world is what's happening, Kasey. It's people feeling free to do what they please without worrying about breaking somebody's stuffy rules. Now, if you think feeling that way makes me a terrible person, then I guess our friendship isn't worth much to you anymore."

"That's not true, Diana. Our friendship is very important to me."

Diana pulled onto the winding road that led to the Carlone farm. "Let's face it, Kasey. Living by the letter of the law is easier for you than it is for me. I'm not like you. It's taken me a long time to realize I can't be a carbon copy of you. I'm not Little Miss Perfect. I have to find what's right for me."

"Well, I'm certainly not Little Miss Perfect either," protested Kasey. "I make mistakes all the time."

"Right. Like maybe you forgot to say please or thank you once, or you stepped on a crack in the sidewalk. Being good just comes natural to you."

"What is it—do you think I'm judging you, looking down on you?"

"Aren't you? You think I was wrong to drink those wine coolers, don't you?"

"All right, since you ask, I don't think it pleases the Lord."

"That's what I mean. I'm tired of trying to please everyone else, especially God. I want to please *me* for a change. But that makes me an evil person, doesn't it?"

"I didn't say that, Diana."

"No, but if I did something unthinkable, like have sex or smoke pot or try crack, you'd think I was an evil person, right?"

"That's a loaded question, but—OK, I would think you were heading for trouble. Is that what you're doing,

Diana—having sex? Or is it—are you—you're not taking drugs, are you?"

Diana swerved her car into the Carlone driveway and gunned the engine. "Do you really think I'd do something stupid like that? Come on, I was just tossing out some examples." Diana stopped near the screened porch and watched solemnly as Kasey climbed out. "You're still going to work at the Emporium, aren't you, Kasey?"

"Of course. But I can't work Sunday—"

"You mean, you *won't* work Sunday."

"OK. I won't work Sunday, but I'll be there Monday morning as soon as I finish my chores and piano practice."

Diana smiled grudgingly. "See you then." She paused and added, "Your music made a hit with my friends, for what it's worth."

Kasey grinned. "I'm glad. And for what it's worth, I didn't dislike your friends, OK?"

That night, after Grams and Gramps had gone to bed, Kasey couldn't sleep, so she slipped outside and walked around the house to the barn. She climbed up on the old oak fence and gazed at the stars.

From the time she first asked Jesus into her life, Kasey loved sitting out under the stars at night and talking aloud to God. He seemed so near, and the whole world grew hushed as they carried on their private conversation. At least, that's how it seemed to Kasey.

Aloud she said, "Jesus, I'm really confused. Should I have said more about You to the people at Sonja's party? Or was I too critical? Did I alienate Diana for no reason? Should I have taken more of a stand for You? Did I blow it? If I get caught in a situation like that again, how do I know what to say or what not to say?"

"Excuse me. Are you talking to someone?"

Kasey whirled around in alarm, nearly toppling off the fence.

It was Dusty, standing by the barn, half his face silhouetted by shadows, the other half awash in moonlight.

"Oh, Dusty, you scared me out of my wits!"

"Sorry, Kasey. I heard voices—uh, one voice, I guess. There's no one else here that I can see."

Kasey felt her face redden with embarrassment. "I—I was talking to the Lord."

"The Lord. You mean, as in heaven?"

"Uh, yeah. We do this—I mean, I do this a lot—talk to God about my problems and things. I suppose that sounds weird if you haven't gotten to know Him yourself—"

"Gotten to know him?"

"The Lord."

Dusty chuckled self-consciously. "I don't rightly recall being introduced. I'm sure I'd remember if I'd made His acquaintance. A guy wouldn't forget sitting down for a chat with the Almighty."

"Are you making fun of me?"

"No way, Kasey. I'm just—I don't know—I never met anyone who sat out on a fence at night talking to God like He was just an ordinary Joe—"

"Oh, He's not. He's not ordinary at all. He's the God of the whole universe!"

"And He's here right now talking to you on this fence?"

Kasey nodded. "He talks to me wherever I am."

Dusty sauntered over and sat beside her on the fence. "Can I hear Him? I mean, if I get real quiet and listen?"

Kasey eyed him skeptically. "Get real, Dusty. He speaks to me in my heart, not out loud. You are making fun of me, aren't you!"

"I swear to you I'm not. I'm just—fascinated. I never met anyone like you, Kasey, with such simple faith. I'm trying to figure out what makes you tick."

"It's not me. It's Jesus in me. His Spirit."

"Now we're talking spirits?"

Kasey sighed. "I'm digging myself in deeper, aren't I? What I'm trying to say is that when I asked Jesus into my life, His Spirit came to live inside me. If you see something different in me, it's because of Him."

Dusty reached over and squeezed her arm. "You're OK, kid. We could all use a dose of what you've got. The world would be a better place."

"It's free," said Kasey.

"What's free?" He eyed her curiously.

"What I've got."

"Oh, you mean this religious thing?"

"No, I mean a relationship with God. All you have to do is ask and Jesus will come into your life too."

Dusty chuckled uneasily. "My life's not too pretty, Kasey. In fact, it's a royal mess. God wouldn't like slumming it."

"He 'slums it' for all of us. We've all done bad things, Dusty, but God loves us anyway. That's why Jesus died on the cross. He paid the penalty for us so we would be free to get to know God. That's why I can sit here on this fence under the stars and talk to Him and know He's listening."

Dusty shook his head. "I don't want to bust your bubble, but nothing's that good, Kasey. And nobody."

"Jesus is. I've spent most of my life getting to know Him."

"Well, gal, I've spent most of my life getting to know a side of life you can't even imagine, and I figure if there's a God, He would have cleaned all that stuff up a long time ago."

Dusty eased himself off the fence, then held out his arms and lifted Kasey down. For a moment he stood facing her, his hands still on her waist. "But if anything was ever going to make me believe, kiddo, you're probably the one. You're one special gal."

Kasey gazed up at him, spellbound by his eyes. She couldn't move, could scarcely breathe. His touch was electric, his closeness mesmerizing. It occurred to her that he might kiss her. The idea sent chills up her spine. She thought, *I'm going to die. I'm simply going to die.*

But then he released her and stepped back into the shadows and said, "You better go inside, Kasey. It's getting late."

She nodded and broke into a run for the house. She wasn't sure what had just happened or what it all meant, but she knew she would never forget these past ten minutes with Dusty for the rest of her life.

11

As the warm, muggy days of summer slipped by, Kasey fell into a predictable routine. She rose early each morning and fixed breakfast for her grandparents, tidied the farmhouse, spent an hour chatting with her grandmother, prepared lunch, practiced piano for an hour, then rode her bicycle into town for an afternoon of work at the Emporium. She had finally managed to call it that—Emporium—without feeling repulsed. And even though the store was vastly different from her father's old general store, she discovered she loved working there as much as before.

Maybe it was the people. Certainly, it was the people. She was becoming acquainted with them all over again, and she could sense that she had regained her place in their hearts. She thrived on their smiles and words of appreciation and loved helping them find just the right thing they were looking for. And how often they told her, "Kasey, it's great having you back!"

After dinner each evening, Kasey spent some time alone on the screened porch or strolling around the farm. It was the best time of the day to talk to the Lord, with a cool breeze stirring and the crickets chirping and the stars as bright as diamonds on a bed of blue velvet. Kasey loved the farm and savored the fragrances of honeysuckle and freshly cut hay. She even loved the damp, rich smell of the earth just after a thunderstorm.

Some evenings Dusty joined her, sitting on the fence to chat or lingering on the porch after supper. Kasey looked forward to those times with Dusty, and yet the undercurrent of excitement she felt in his presence was always tinged with a sense of foreboding. She couldn't find words to explain it, just as she couldn't articulate her feelings for Dusty. They were so different from what she felt for Ryan, and yet she realized her fondness for Dusty was growing stronger every day.

One afternoon when Kasey and Diana were both working in the Emporium, Dusty came in with a long list of supplies he needed. Kasey took the list and smiled, until she realized Dusty and Diana were staring each other down.

"Uh, I don't think you two have met, have you?" she asked tentatively. "Diana, Dusty Jernigan—Dusty, Diana Morley."

"Hi," Dusty grunted.

"Hello, Dusty," Diana purred.

"Dusty works for us," Kasey explained. "He's Gramps's hired man."

"Yes, I saw him that time I brought you home, Kasey," Diana said nonchalantly. She looked up at Dusty. "How long have you been in Middleton, Dusty?"

"Not long."

"I'm surprised I haven't seen you around town before this."

"I come in when I need to."

"He's awfully busy on the farm," said Kasey. "He does a terrific job."

"I bet he does," said Diana, her gaze still appraising him. "Where are you from, Dusty?"

"Nowhere special."

Diana laughed. "Oh, come on, everybody's from *some*where."

He shrugged. "You could say I'm from *every*where."

"You planning to stay in Middleton?" Diana asked, sounding a little impatient now.

"Maybe, maybe not." He took a step back. "Excuse me, Miss Morley, I better look up these items. I'm due back at the farm."

"Fine, but it's *Diana*. Miss Morley sounds so stuffy."

Dusty grinned for the first time. "I can see you're not that."

"We'll help you find the supplies," said Kasey, already heading for the first item on the list.

"Sure, I'll help too," said Diana off-handedly.

After Dusty had gone, Diana flashed Kasey a knowing smile. "You like him, don't you?"

"Who?" Kasey asked, knowing exactly who.

"Dusty. I could feel the electricity between you two."

"You could not!" cried Kasey. "We're only friends."

"But it could be more, couldn't it? You two could have something real hot going on between you."

Kasey felt a ground swell of anger rise inside her, a geyser of outraged indignation. "If you don't know me better than that, Diana, then I don't know how we were ever best friends!"

Diana waved a conciliatory hand. "Whoa, I never said anything was going on. I just said I felt the vibes."

Kasey sighed, quelling the waves of roiling emotion threatening to spill over. "You know I already have a boyfriend," she declared. "Ryan and I write each other all the time."

"Fine," said Diana. "I'm glad you're not interested in someone like this Dusty character."

Kasey paused. "What do you mean, 'this Dusty character'?"

Diana wiped a streak of dust from the countertop and blew it off her finger. "I just mean, I wouldn't trust Dusty Jernigan any farther than I could throw him."

"Why not?" demanded Kasey.

"Because you don't know the first thing about him. Do you? You told me your grandfather hired him without even checking his background. Has he told you anything about himself? Where he's from? Who his family is?"

"No," Kasey admitted, "except that he's had a rough life."

"Did he explain what he meant? Give any details?"

"No. Except that his mother drank too much."

"A rough life could mean anything, Kasey. He acts like someone with something to hide. He's suspicious and standoffish. Maybe he's in trouble with the law. Maybe he's an ex-con. He could be a hatchet murderer for all we know."

Kasey heaved an exasperated sigh. "Get real, Diana. You watch too much TV. I'm sure Dusty hasn't done anything wrong."

"But you don't know for sure, do you?"

"OK, I don't know for sure."

Diana folded her hands across her chest. "I rest my case."

When Kasey got home from work that evening, she sought Dusty out. He was in the barn, repairing a saddle. He must have heard her footsteps in the crackling hay because he whirled around with an abruptness that startled her. "Oh, it's you, Kasey," he said.

"Who did you think it was?"

"Nobody." He shrugged and put down the saddle. "Looking for something?"

"No. Just thought I'd make sure you got all the stuff on your list."

"Yeah. You did good."

She pulled a sheath of straw from the loft and traced the rough grain of the wood. "What did you think of my friend Diana?"

Dusty managed a crooked grin. "Nothing."

"Nothing? You mean you have no opinion?"

"She's pretty. Snobbish. Not as nice as you."

Kasey smiled. "Thanks—I guess. She asked about you."

Dusty brushed straw off his Levi's. "What for?"

"I don't know. She was just curious."

Irritation stole into his voice. "I hope you told her to mind her own business."

"Of course not. She's my best friend. Besides," Kasey said softly, "I wonder too. How come you never talk about yourself, Dusty? Why don't you let people get to know you?"

He sat down on a bale of straw and propped one foot against another bale. Kasey sat down beside him. Neither of them spoke for a minute. Kasey wasn't sure whether she should stay or leave, whether he was angry with her or ready to talk. She just knew she had to pursue this conversation until she got some answers.

"I don't like people much," Dusty said at last. "I've never been able to trust 'em. I figure the less people know about me, the better off I am. When they know too much about you, they can use it to cut your throat. When they get too close, they can stab you in the back."

Kasey looked up at him. "Do you feel that way about me, too?"

He reached over and put a piece of straw in her hair.

"Naw. You're OK. I never met anyone like you."

"Then why can't you trust me? Why can't you talk to me?"

"Why? What would it accomplish?"

"I don't know. Maybe then you'd know you're not alone. That people care about you. God cares about you."

"People care? God cares? How about you, Kasey? How do you feel about me?"

Kasey looked away, flustered. "I—I care too, Dusty."

"Like this?" he asked. He pulled her into his arms and brought his mouth down on her lips.

She reacted with panic, pushing him away and dashing out of the barn. Even when he called after her, she ran all the way into the house without looking back.

With the door closed soundly behind her, she felt suddenly foolish and embarrassed. She didn't know whether to be angry at Dusty for surprising her with his sudden passion or angry at herself for giving him the chance to kiss her and then running away like a frightened child. And she was frightened, she realized. But she wasn't sure which she feared more: Dusty's volatile emotions or her own.

Kasey was still trembling when the telephone rang moments later. It was Mr. Morley from the Emporium. "Sorry to bother you, Kasey," he said, "but we've run into a little problem here at the store. The books don't balance right tonight. We're missing a hundred dollars. Can you come up with any explanation?"

"No, no, I can't, Mr. Morley. Are you sure the money is missing? Could you have made an error in your figures?"

"No, I checked it several times. There's no mistake. We're a hundred dollars short."

"I'm so sorry. I—I wish I could help, Mr. Morley—"

"Thanks, Kasey. Let's just hope it doesn't happen again."

12

But it did happen again. A week later, $200 was missing from the Emporium's register. Two days later, another store in town reported a theft, and a week later, another store. Three days after that, the Emporium was hit again. This time, $300 was missing.

The town buzzed with suspicion and fear. Who would be hit next? Who was able to sneak into the merchants' cash registers without their awareness? Who would do such a thing? And how?

"There's nobody in this town who would pull such a stunt," Mr. Morley told Kasey one afternoon. "We've all known one another all our lives. And there've been no strangers in town, nobody suspicious. It's a real mystery to me."

"But, Daddy, there is a stranger in town," said Diana. "He's been here all along, before the robberies started."

"Who?" demanded Mr. Morley.

Kasey already knew the answer, and so did Mr. Morley.

"You mean that hired hand out at the Carlone farm?" Mr. Morley looked at Kasey. "That hired man of yours —Dusty what's-his-name—do you think he could be doing this?"

"No, of course not," Kasey declared. "I'm sure he'd never do such a terrible thing."

"But who else, Daddy?" said Diana. "He comes into town regularly for supplies. I bet he's been in all the stores that have been robbed."

"Well, if he has, I'm going to find out about it—and pronto!" Mr. Morley stomped out of the store, his eyes blazing fire.

Kasey looked at Diana. "Do you really think it was Dusty?"

She shrugged. "You tell me, Kasey. Who else could it be?"

That evening, Mr. Morley paid Grandpa Carlone a visit. Kasey was in the kitchen washing dishes, but she could hear the two men talking in the living room. Mr. Morley was obviously upset.

"I don't want to go behind your back with this thing, Tonio. I figure you got a right to know. There's been a rash of petty robberies in town. The merchants suspect your hired man. He's made purchases at all the stores that were hit, so he had access."

"So has nearly everyone else in town," protested Grandpa Carlone. "What makes you suspect Dusty?"

"I'll tell you straight out. He's a stranger, a loner, and nobody, including you, knows a thing about him. Besides, we figure it would take a pretty smooth operator to pull off these thefts with no one the wiser. That takes a professional. You know any professional crooks in this community, Tonio?"

"All I know is my man wouldn't steal."

"Well, sure, it's a hard pill to swallow, finding out the man you trusted is a thief, but—"

"You got proof of that, Morley?"

"No, but let's face it, who else would it be?"

"I don't know. But it wasn't Dusty. Now I'll thank you to keep your accusations to yourself unless you come up with proof to back up your claims."

Grandfather Carlone walked Mr. Morley to the door. Kasey caught a glimpse of them. She could tell Mr. Morley was more than a little angry. "I'm sorry you feel this way, Tonio. We—the other merchants and I—were hoping you'd cooperate with us in running this no-good out of town."

"He's my man, Morley. I'll be responsible for him."

"That mean you'll pay us for what he steals?"

"You bring me proof he's your man, and I'll make it good what he's taken."

"We'll get the proof, Tonio. You'll see. You're a blind fool to trust that drifter."

Shortly after Mr. Morley left, Dusty appeared at the door. "Your granddad busy?" he asked Kasey.

"No, he's in the living room. In fact, I think he was about to go find you."

Dusty frowned. "Yeah, that's what I was afraid of."

While Dusty went on to the living room, Kasey lingered over the dishwater. It wasn't that she intended to eavesdrop on her grandfather's conversation, but if she happened to overhear what they were saying, she would be better prepared to help Dusty.

She heard Dusty say, "I guess you want me to pack up and get out, Mr. Carlone?"

"Any reason I should?" asked Gramps.

"I heard the rumors, sir. I know what they're saying about me in town. And I saw Mr. Morley leave here a few minutes ago. I know he's after my hide."

"You know why, Dusty?"

"He thinks I stole his money."

"Did you?"

"No, sir."

"Then that's all I needed to know. You go back to work, Dusty."

"That's it? I'm not fired? You believe me?"

"That's right, Dusty. You've never given me any reason not to trust you. As long as you behave yourself, you got a job with me."

Dusty was beaming when he came back out to the kitchen. "Your granddad's an OK guy, you know that, Kasey?"

She turned to him, wiping her hands on a dish towel. "I've known that for as long as I can remember." She nodded toward a pie on the table. "You want some cherry pie and ice cream?"

He grinned. "Yeah. I feel like celebrating!"

Kasey and Dusty lingered at the kitchen table for over an hour eating their pie, chatting, and laughing. Gramps peeked in once to say he and Grams were hitting the sack. Then, except for the radio droning "Blueberry Hill" in slow, melodic tones, the house was quiet.

Finally, Dusty pushed his chair back from the table and said, "I guess I'd better get back out to the bunkhouse."

Kasey followed him out to the porch. They stood there for a moment in the shadows, breathing in the fragrant summer air. "Can you smell Grams's roses on the trellis over there?" she whispered.

"Yep. And I can smell rain in the air. It'll hit maybe about midnight and give us a good drenching."

Kasey sat down on the edge of the swing. "I love how it smells just before the rain. It's like the earth and all the growing things just fill up your senses. Don't you love it?"

"I sure do." He sat down beside her. "That's why I'll never take an indoor job. I like working close to the earth, feeling the sun on my back, the soil under my feet, the crops in my hand. You know, you can trust the land when you can't trust people."

"Some people you can trust," said Kasey.

He looked at her. "I know. Like you and your grandparents. That's why I've stayed this long."

"You usually keep moving on?"

"Yeah. Usually after a few weeks."

"How come?"

"I figure it's best not to get too tangled up with people. Hang loose, that's my motto."

Kasey studied Dusty's face—the way the moonlight caught the planes and angles of his nose and chin. "Someone must have hurt you once a whole lot," she murmured.

He was silent.

"I wish I could help, Dusty."

"You do. By being here. By being you."

"If you ever want to talk about it—"

"What good would it do?"

"Sometimes it makes me feel better just talking stuff over with my mom or Grams. Maybe you'd feel better too."

He sat forward and rested his chin in his hands. "Nothing I say can change anything."

"What would you change?"

"Nothing. There's nothing I can change."

"But if you could—"

He sat back and ran his fingers through the thatch of hair on his forehead. Softly he said, "I'd bring my little brother back."

Kasey looked intently at him. "What? Your brother?"

"Yeah. Danny. He was five. Just a little kid."

"What happened to him?"

73

"He died."

"I'm sorry," said Kasey.

"Yeah, well, he shouldn't have died. It was my fault."

"Your fault? How?"

"I should have been there for him. I should have protected him."

"Protected him from what?"

"From my dad."

The words caught in Kasey's throat. "Y-Your dad?"

Haltingly, Dusty told his story. "My dad was a drinker just like my mom. Only booze made him mean. Real mean. I could take his beatings. Sometimes I even fought back. But not Danny. He was so little. And scared. I always told him I'd take care of him. I wouldn't let Dad hurt him. So whenever Dad laid into Danny, I always teed him off and got him swinging at me instead. That way, he left Danny alone."

"Couldn't you have got help, called the police?"

"Sure. So they take my old man off to jail. Who buys the food, who pays the rent? My mom was sick a lot. She couldn't work. She said, 'As long as your dad pays the bills, you be a man and take whatever he dishes out.' So I did."

"But what about Danny?"

Dusty cupped his hands behind his head and stared up into the darkness. "Yeah, that's what I'm getting to." His voice grew gravelly with emotion. "One night I was out, bumming around, not doing much, you know, and I come home, and everything's quiet. Mom's sitting in a chair like a zombie, Dad's passed out on the couch, and I got this feeling something's wrong. I go to the bedroom and turn on the light, and I see Danny in his bed asleep. And I figure all is cool, right? Only I go over to him and touch his face, like I'm going to kiss him good night, you know? Only—only his cheek is cold. And then I see the bruises on his head and the blood on his pillow, and I go crazy. I know he's dead, only I won't accept it. I pick him up in my arms and hug him and beg him to come back. But it's too late!"

"Oh, Dusty!"

Somehow—Kasey wasn't sure who made the first move—but they were in each other's arms, and even though Dusty didn't make a sound, she could feel his tears on her cheek. They sat that way for a long while before she asked, "What did you do, Dusty?"

He released her, pulled a handkerchief from his back pocket, and mopped his eyes. "I got out of there fast. I knew if I stayed I'd kill my dad. I started running, and I've been running ever since, and that's what I'll probably do for the rest of my life."

"You mean, you never found out what happened?"

"I read about it in the papers. My dad went to prison."

"But you never went home again?"

"What for? Danny was the only decent thing in my life. And he was gone."

"But your mom—maybe she needs you. Maybe she's changed."

"People don't change, Kasey. Once a loser, always a loser."

"That's not true. God can change people—if they let Him."

Dusty smiled and drew her over against him. "That's what I love about you, Kasey. Your absolute faith in God and people."

She looked up at him. "People can let you down, but not God. He loves you, Dusty, and He wants the best for you."

"I wish I could believe that, but so far I haven't seen much evidence of God's love in my life."

"Maybe you just haven't been looking for it. Maybe His love has been there waiting for you all the time."

Dusty bent over and kissed her forehead. "If anybody could make me believe that, Kasey, it'd be you." Carefully he removed her glasses and ran his finger over her nose and chin. "You make me feel loved, Kasey. I haven't felt that way for a long, long time."

She could smell the cherry pie on his breath as he brought his face close to hers. She knew she should get up and run into the house, but she couldn't make herself move. Then it was too late. His lips were on hers, and he was crushing her against him.

Panic soared inside her, edged out by sensations she had never known she could feel. Passion. Desire. Dusty wasn't just kissing her now; she was kissing him. She felt as if the whole world had ebbed away and there was no one on earth but the two of them.

But when she felt Dusty fumbling with her clothing, she reacted instinctively and pushed him away.

"No, Dusty!"

"Please, Kasey, I need you!"

She jumped up, bolted for the screen door and slammed it behind her. She ran through the dark house to her room and threw herself on the bed, burying her face in her pillow. Despairingly she thought, *Oh, God, I only wanted to help Dusty. Now I've ruined everything!*

13

Kasey couldn't sleep that night. She kept thinking about Dusty and Ryan—two boys she cared deeply about who were so vastly different from each other. Guilt weighed on her heart like a great rock. She couldn't erase from her mind the moments she'd just spent with Dusty, nor could she deny the surprising power of her feelings. Did it mean she loved Dusty, or just that he had stirred something in her that she had never permitted with Ryan? Actually, Ryan had never put her in a position of having to tell him no. She had loved that about Ryan, the fact that he respected her and was careful not to let their kisses get too passionate.

But Dusty. He was another story. Why hadn't she kept her guard up? Why hadn't she recognized the compromising situation she was getting herself into? Or was it that she simply hadn't listened to her own common sense, to the still, small voice of her conscience?

Somewhere inside herself, she had sensed that Dusty would make advances, that he was vulnerable and she was vulnerable. And yet, it hadn't mattered. Why? She knew, if she was honest with herself, that she wanted Dusty to hold her and kiss her. She wanted to be close to him, to feel his touch. And even when she pushed him away, she really wanted to stay.

That night, as Kasey tossed and turned, she realized she had never really had a guilty conscience before—at least not like this. Oh, she had made little mistakes that had caused fleeting pangs of remorse, like when she mouthed off to her mom or got in a verbal battle with her brother, Keith. But those times were small change compared with this. She felt as if a wall had shot up blocking her relationship with Ryan and, even worse, blocking her relationship with the Lord.

Would the Lord stop being her best Friend because she had sexual feelings and desires? Of course not! He understood. Wasn't sex His idea in the first place? At least, sex in the context of marriage. And He would understand how weak she was, wouldn't He? And forgive her for getting carried away with Dusty?—even if she still felt too ashamed to ask for His forgiveness?

But what plagued Kasey most was the realization that she had stepped inadvertently into a whole new arena of life—the sexual arena, a brand new field of conflict and temptation. She had caught a glimpse of what it could be like, had had the briefest taste. What if it all happened again? What if she found herself in Dusty's arms some other time? Would she lose the battle? How would she keep these strong feelings under control? Would she be able to run away next time?

And how could she feel this way about Dusty when she was so sure she loved Ryan? Was she really fickle at heart? All of her life she had carried an image in her mind of who and what Kasey Carlone was. Proper, prudent, trustworthy, predictable. Now, suddenly, because of Dusty, that image was up for grabs. She wasn't sure anymore exactly who Kasey Carlone was or what she might do in certain circumstances.

Was this how it was for girls who got in trouble, girls who became promiscuous or got pregnant? Did it happen before they even realized they could be that kind of girl?

Kasey got out of bed and walked over to the window. She stared out at the stars. They were as sparkling bright as ever. Usually, during moments like this, she would feel a warm swell of emotion for the Lord, and she would pour out her feelings to Him. But tonight, with Dusty's kisses still fresh on her lips, there was this niggling breach between them.

She knew God had promised never to leave her or forsake her, so the problem had to be on her end. She had violated her conscience, and now her guilt was erecting a roadblock between her and the Lord.

"Dear Jesus, I don't want to feel this way," she whispered. "I want to feel close to You again. Forgive me for letting things get too involved with Dusty. I know You want me to be his friend and tell him about Your love. And I know if we get sidetracked with sex, it'll spoil everything—for both of us. Help me to do what's right. Help me remember that sex is Your special gift for a husband and wife to share. Don't let me throw that precious gift away for a few moments of pleasure with Dusty."

When Kasey slipped back into bed, she knew everything was OK again with the Lord. That was the great thing about being a Christian. Even when she did something wrong, Jesus was ready to forgive her and help her make things right. But she sensed God had a big job in store for Him when it came to her feelings for Dusty. Dusty had suffered so much pain in his life. He needed someone to care for him. Who else was there but Kasey? She felt sorry for him and wanted to comfort him. But Jesus would have to make her strong enough to keep Dusty at arm's length.

The next day, Kasey considered telling Grams and Gramps about her dilemma with Dusty. But, then again, with the townspeople convinced Dusty was stealing from them, she didn't want to stir up any more questions or controversy. So she kept last night to herself.

Her grandparents were preoccupied with their own concerns anyway. Grams was in a wheelchair now and just learning to use a walker. She was excited about her new mobility and eager to get back into her former routine. Kasey had to shoo her out of the kitchen to be sure she didn't overdo. "That hip's still mending," she said more than once, echoing what both the doctor and visiting nurse had told Grams time and again.

Gramps was glad to see Grams on her feet again, even if only briefly with the help of a walker. But he had his own worries that kept him from entering fully into Grams's excitement. Gramps was having serious problems with his tractor. He'd known for a long time that it would need to be replaced someday, and he'd been saving every dime and nickel he could lay his hands on. Now, at last, he figured maybe he had enough.

So while Kasey debated about whether to confide in her grandparents about Dusty, Gramps was sitting at the kitchen table counting out the cash in his strongbox. "I've got me close to $2,000," he told Kasey. "If I can foot a loan at the bank, maybe I can buy that tractor. How'd you like to go someday soon and help me pick one out?"

"Sure, Gramps. Whenever you say."

"Maybe next week. How's your work schedule at the Emporium?"

"I work every afternoon except Wednesday."

"OK, how about Wednesday then?"

Before Kasey could reply, there was a knock at the door. To Kasey's surprise, it was Diana, holding a handful of mail. "Hi, Kasey, I met the postman on my way to the door. Here you are."

"Come on in, Diana. Sit down." Kasey glanced through the mail. *Oh no, a letter from Ryan. Of all days!*

"Oh ho, a letter from that boyfriend of yours, huh, Kasey?" said Gramps as he replaced the money in his strongbox.

"Do we get to hear it?" asked Diana in a teasing, sing-song voice.

"Maybe. After I read it." Kasey tucked it in her shirt pocket. "Later, OK?"

"Sure," said Diana. "But, listen, Kasey, we need to talk."

"OK, let's go to my room. Excuse us, Gramps."

"You two go on. I know how it is with girl talk."

They went to Kasey's room, and she shut the door behind them.

"I can't believe it," said Diana, sitting down on the bed.

"What?" asked Kasey.

"That your grandfather would keep so much cash around when he has a known thief on the premises."

"Gramps doesn't believe Dusty's a thief," said Kasey defensively.

"Well, if you ask me, he's tempting fate by being so trusting."

"That isn't what you came to tell me, is it, Diana?"

"No. I came to ask if you'd like to drive to Bloomington with me Friday night."

"You're spending another weekend with Sonja?"

"Why not? We have a blast."

"Don't your parents think you spend too much time there?"

"Why should they? It's summer. My time's my own, except when I'm working at the store. So how about it? Wanna join me?"

"No, thanks. I'm helping Grams with her therapy, and besides, I'm scheduled to work at the store Saturday."

Diana held out her hand and examined her long, polished nails. "Uh, no, you're not, Kasey. Dad assigned those hours to someone else."

"Why? He knows I love the work."

Diana looked at her with a sad little pout. "I didn't want to tell you this, Kasey, but I guess it's better you hear it from me than from someone else."

"Hear what?"

"The rumor mill in town. It's working overtime again."

"What do you mean?"

"Well, you know we had more money missing from the Emporium about a week ago?"

"Uh, yes, I was there. It was about $50, wasn't it?"

"Yes, and my poor father is absolutely beside himself. I've never seen him so upset. I mean, we just don't know where it's all going to end."

"I know." Kasey sighed. "You want me to talk Gramps into getting rid of Dusty, but honestly, Diana, I just can't—"

"No, that's not it. People are starting to say something else, Kasey."

"What are they saying?"

"That—maybe—I'm so sorry, Kasey—but they're saying maybe you're the one taking the money."

Kasey jumped up off the bed. "Me? You're kidding!"

"No, Kasey. It's not everyone, you understand. Most people don't believe it for a minute. But there are a few rather vocal folks who are wondering if you might be the thief."

"Why would they think that?" demanded Kasey.

Diana's forehead puckered a little as if the words pained her to say them. "You were working at the Emporium all the times it was robbed. That doesn't prove anything, of course. But some people are wondering if maybe you changed when you went away to Springfield. They say, 'How do we know she's the same sweet, sincere girl?'"

Kasey felt tears sting her eyes. "I can't believe it. I can't believe people would really think that of me."

"Oh, don't get me wrong, Kasey. For every person who raises such questions, a dozen people come to your defense. Like I said, it's just a few bad-mouthers."

Tears ran down Kasey's cheeks. "It doesn't matter if it's a few or a hundred. If people think I'm guilty of such a terrible crime—"

"Well, that's what my daddy said. He said keeping you on might be bad for business. He said people might think you and Dusty are in cahoots, working together, you know, what with him living here at your place and all."

"Your father actually said that—?"

"Well, he's not showing a lick of sense, of course, and I all but told him so, but I can't very well tell him how to run his business, now can I?"

Kasey wiped her eyes with a tissue. "Are you saying I'm out of a job? Your dad doesn't want me back at the Emporium?"

Diana reached for a tissue too. "My allergies," she murmured.

"I asked you a question," said Kasey. "Am I out of work?"

"Only temporarily. Just until these crimes get solved. Once people aren't so edgy anymore, Dad will be glad to have you back."

"But I'll only be in Middleton a few more weeks anyway. The summer's almost over."

Diana sighed audibly. "My dad says if your grandfather gets rid of Dusty Jernigan, he'll take you back at the store no matter what anybody says."

"But that's not fair. Gramps believes Dusty. He's already told him he can stay."

Diana stood up and reached for the doorknob. "Then your grandfather's a fool, Kasey, and if he's not careful, he'll be Dusty's victim just like the rest of us!"

14

After Diana left, Kasey remained in her room for a long while mulling over her various dilemmas. She was suddenly out of a job, and how could she possibly explain the reason to her grandparents? It was incredible that the townspeople were beginning to suspect she was a thief— or at least the friend of a thief! How was she to extricate herself from such a predicament?

And then there was Dusty. She was terribly attracted to him, but he was all wrong for her. Most important, he didn't share her faith in Jesus. And, of course, they had so little in common. Yet, because of last night he was probably expecting more from her now than she could ever give. She had no idea how to tell Ryan back home about her feelings for Dusty. Did she even owe him an explanation?

And now that her feelings about Ryan and Dusty were totally confused, here was a letter from Ryan that would surely remind her of her guilt.

She tore open the envelope and reluctantly began to read:

Dear Kasey,

    I haven't heard from you lately, so I assume you're very busy helping your grandparents and working at the store. You must feel very good about doing so many productive things with your summer. I'm sure your grandparents are grateful to have you helping them.

    I know how grateful I'll be to have you home again. Just think. Only a few more weeks and you'll be back and everything will be just as it was before. I hope you're counting the days as much as I am. By the way, you don't have to worry about me looking at other girls. I only have eyes for you.

    Everything is OK here. Work is a drag as usual, but I'm socking my money away so we can have some good times this fall. Maybe we'll go to that fancy restaurant out by the mall when you get back—the one where the menus are all in French. We'll celebrate being together again, and next time I won't let you go so far away.

    Everyone at Shady Oaks misses you and asks when you'll be back. They all know what a special girl you are, and I know it too. All your friends miss you, but I miss you most of all. Please write!

Love always,
Ryan

Kasey set the letter aside and removed her glasses. They were getting misty from her tears. Poor Ryan! He was so trusting. What would he say if he knew she had been in another man's arms and kissed in a way Ryan had never kissed her? She had worried so much about Ryan's finding another girl while she was gone, but it had never occurred to her that she could be attracted to another guy. How could things ever be the same when she returned to

Springfield? Would Ryan understand if she told him what happened? Would she still feel the same about Ryan? Or would her heart still be here in Middleton with Dusty?

Kasey put Ryan's letter away and wondered what had happened to the days when life seemed so uncomplicated, when everything was either black or white, good or bad, right or wrong? Lately, there seemed to be no easy choices, no obvious course of action. No matter what she did there would be repercussions and more dilemmas. So what was a girl to do?

Kasey figured she'd better start by letting her grandparents know she was out of a job. She found them in the living room. Gramps was working on some bills, while Grams was watching an old "Lucy" rerun on TV. Kasey waited for the commercial, then told them what had happened as simply as she could.

Grandpa Carlone was livid. "You mean, people in town have the gall to accuse you of stealing? Where in thunder have they checked their brains? Don't they know an honest, God-fearing child when they see one? I'll drive into town and give them a piece of my mind."

"Now, Tonio, keep calm," said Grams, "before you have a heart attack or a stroke. One of us on the mend is enough."

"But, Emma, how can I sit back and watch them malign our granddaughter? Something's got to be done!"

"They said—" Kasey hesitated.

"Yes, Kasey, my girl. Tell me what they said."

"They said—I mean, Mr. Morley said—if you get rid of Dusty, I can keep my job."

"Why, that sounds like blackmail to me. I'd like to horsewhip the whole bunch of 'em!"

"No, dear," said Grams, "that won't solve anything."

"All right, Emma, what will? You tell me!"

She shook her head. "Heavens, I only wish I knew."

"Well, I don't like being backed in a corner, especially when it concerns my granddaughter—"

"What are you going to do, Gramps?" asked Kasey.

Her grandfather cleared his throat noisily. "I'm going to tell Dusty he has to go. I can't let his presence tear apart our family and ruin your good name in this town."

"No, Gramps, it hasn't. It won't. Please don't send him away. If you do, he'll never believe anyone cares about him. He'll keep running and be miserable for the rest of his life."

"Now, you don't know that."

"Yes, I do. Please let him stay, Gramps."

"I have another concern, Kasey," Gramps admitted, talking confidentially now. "What if the townspeople are right about Dusty? What if he has been taking money from the merchants? I'm a stubborn old man, and I defended him partly because I didn't want to admit I'd made a mistake in hiring him. But people are right—we don't know the first thing about that boy. I don't want to be exposing you and your grandmother to someone who might be committing a crime. If it turns out he's guilty, we could all be in danger."

"No, Gramps. Dusty isn't guilty. And he wouldn't hurt any of us. I know him. And you're a good judge of character. You know in your heart that he wouldn't steal from anybody. Please don't fire him."

Her grandfather shook his head ponderously. "I just don't know, Kasey. But if you believe in him and feel so strongly that he should stay, who am I to send him away?"

"Thanks, Gramps," said Kasey.

"Tell you what, Kasey, my girl—" Her grandfather walked over to the linen closet and opened the door. He reached in to the back and brought out his strongbox. "If you're going to be out of a job, I'm going to give you a little spending money to carry around with you." He handed her $20. "Think that'll tide you over for a few days?"

She pushed the money back into his hand. "No, Gramps, you don't have to give me your money. You're saving that for your new tractor. I'm fine. You already give me everything I need. I don't need spending money."

"Sure you do. For sodas and makeup and all that stuff girls buy. You take it."

"OK, but I'm still going to talk to Mr. Morley. Maybe he was just saying that stuff about me losing my job to force you to fire Dusty."

"Uh-hem, did I hear my name?"

Kasey whirled around and looked toward the screen door. Dusty was standing there on the porch, about to knock. Kasey hurried to the door. "Goodness, Dusty, we didn't hear you come up the steps." She opened the door for him. "Come on in. Gramps and I were just, uh, talking business."

He smiled. "Well, my ears weren't burning, so I guess you weren't saying anything too bad."

"Sit a spell and have some lunch with us," called Gramps as he returned his strongbox to the linen closet.

"Thanks, Mr. Carlone, but I just wanted to borrow Kasey for a few minutes, if it's OK with you."

Kasey laughed, puzzled. "Borrow me? What do you mean?"

"I'd like us to talk, Kasey," Dusty said softly. "Can we take a little walk down to the creek?"

"Uh, yeah, I guess so. I'll be back in a little while and fix lunch, OK, Grams?"

"Sure, child, we can wait."

"Now, you be careful, Kasey, my girl," said Gramps.

"Don't worry, I'll be fine," she called back, knowing Gramps was thinking about the worrisome questions they'd just raised about Dusty.

89

Kasey and Dusty took the winding dirt path across the meadow and followed the railroad tracks to the old trestle. "There used to be a watermelon patch near here," she told him. "Every August we'd come down here with a knife and cut us a juicy slice of watermelon right in the patch. It'd run down our faces and arms, but it was the sweetest taste in the whole world."

"I could use a nice cold slice right about now." Dusty laughed.

Kasey held her breath as they crossed the trestle— she hated heights, and she always had a feeling the rickety old bridge might collapse under her feet. But as always, except for some minor creaking, the trestle held their weight. After hiking through a clump of sycamore trees, they came to the creek meandering peacefully among slate-gray rocks and gnarled roots.

"Gramps used to bring my brother, Keith, and me here when we were kids," Kasey told Dusty as she kicked off her sandals and waded into the cool, sandstone-colored water.

"I love this place," said Dusty. "I come here whenever I can and just sit on a rock and think. It's the most peaceful spot in Middleton."

"I feel that way too." Kasey stooped down and splashed some water on her face. "Once, when Keith and I were swimming in the creek, a water moccasin slithered right over my legs. I nearly died."

"I bet you were scared out of your wits."

"I was. I never swam in the creek again without imagining that snake in the water with me. And what was worst of all, my brother would toss ropes and vines at me and scream, 'Watch out, Kasey, there's another water moccasin!'"

Dusty chuckled. "The kind of brother you'd love to kill, right?" His smile faded as he realized the implication of his words.

Kasey knew he was thinking about his own little brother and how maybe he wouldn't have died if Dusty had been there for him.

"You thinking about Danny?" she asked gently.

He nodded. *"A brother you'd love to kill.* It was a stupid thing to say, wasn't it?"

"No. I say things like that all the time. Especially about Keith." She laughed, hoping he would catch her levity, but his frown remained in place.

Kasey slogged back out of the water and wiped her feet on the grass. She and Dusty sat down in the shade of a sprawling sycamore. It occurred to her that maybe she shouldn't have come to this isolated area with Dusty after what happened last night, and after the questions Gramps had raised. But it was too late now. Besides, she sensed something different in Dusty's mood. He was subdued, almost somber. She knew she didn't need to be afraid of him.

"I wanted to talk to you privately," he said. "I wanted to apologize for last night."

She looked up at him. She didn't know what to say.

"I came on too strong. I didn't mean to scare you. I did scare you, didn't I?"

She gazed out toward the creek. "Yeah."

"I'm sorry. I should have realized—I mean, you're a very innocent girl. I'm not used to girls like you. I didn't know they existed anymore."

She looked back at him to see if he was somehow making fun of her, but no, he looked absolutely earnest. "I'm sorry too," she said.

"You're sorry? What for?"

91

Her voice quavered a little. "I felt so bad about your little brother dying, and about you wandering all over the country without a home. I wanted you to know how much I care and how much God cares about you—"

"I'm glad, Kasey. Glad you care."

"But then we started getting close, and my feelings got all jumbled up," she continued, talking faster now. "I knew it wasn't right. I knew God just wanted me to tell you about Him and His love, not get all romantic and involved, but I didn't listen, because I didn't want to stop—"

"Me neither, Kasey," he said tenderly. "I didn't want to stop either. You're like a little angel who stepped right down from heaven. I don't usually talk like this—mushy and soft and gushy, but I gotta say I never knew anyone like you. And if I did, maybe I'd be different. Maybe I wouldn't be roaming aimless and lost." He reached out and took her hand and pulled her close. "You could make a difference for me, Kasey."

"No, not me, Dusty. Not like this," she said, pulling away and scrambling to her feet. "It's God who can make the difference for you! Not me. I'm sorry. I was wrong to come here!" She turned and began to run.

Dusty stood up and brushed off his Levi's. "Kasey, wait! I'm not going to hurt you!"

He sprinted after her and caught up with her moments later. They walked the rest of the way back to the farm in silence. When they reached the farmhouse, he turned to her and asked, "Still friends?"

She reached for the screen door, looked back, and said solemnly, "*Just* friends."

15

Later that evening, as Kasey said good night to her grandmother, she lingered at Grams's bedside, wondering if she should admit how confused she felt about things happening in her life these days. Should she confide her strong feelings for Dusty? Should she tell Grams how angry she felt at the townspeople who questioned her honesty? Grams was always so wise. Maybe she would know what Kasey should do.

Kasey led into it gently. "Grams, did you have lots of problems when you were my age?"

"Problems? Oh, I'm sure I did, though I can't remember exactly what they were now. Why do you ask, dear?"

Kasey chewed thoughtfully on her lower lip. "Because lately it seems like I've got more problems than I can handle. I thought this was going to be a neat, laid-back summer, Grams. I was looking forward to being back in Middleton with you and Gramps, and my friends, and all the people I grew up with. But now I just feel miserable inside."

Grams reached over and squeezed Kasey's hand. "Dear, I know life's not as easy for young folks these days as it was in my day. Why don't you tell me what's making you feel so miserable?"

Slowly, haltingly, Kasey spilled out her hurt over the townspeople's suspicions, her growing affection for Dusty, and her fear of hurting her boyfriend back home.

"Just how serious is it between you and Dusty?" asked Grams.

Lowering her gaze, Kasey told Grams about her evening with Dusty on the porch. "I didn't mean to lead him on, Grams. It just happened, and suddenly I knew I had to make him stop."

"And he did stop—when you said?"

"Yes. I ran in the house. I felt like such a dork. And then I felt so ashamed."

"Well, Kasey, you made a mistake and got more involved than you intended. But when you realized it, you did the right thing. You ran."

"That was the right thing?"

"Yes. The Bible tells us to 'flee youthful lusts,' not to fight them or try to talk ourselves out of them. They're so powerful, the only thing we can do sometimes to save ourselves is to run. And that's just what God expects us to do. Whenever you find yourself in a situation where you're tempted to commit a sexual sin, just run as fast as your legs can carry you."

Kasey stifled a giggle. "Grams, you almost sound like you know what I'm talking about. You weren't tempted like that in your day, were you?"

Grams smiled mysteriously. "Child, your grandfather was quite a Don Juan in his time. He used to sweet-talk me, and there were times when I had to run just like I'm telling you."

"Gramps? He was like—like Dusty?"

"And probably like most of the young men in this world, Kasey. And like many of the young ladies these days, too, who consider themselves 'sexually liberated.'"

Kasey shook her head. "I feel like such an innocent when it comes to dating, Grams. I never had a date until I started going with Ryan, and he's been so considerate, never making demands. So when Dusty came on so strong, I didn't know how to handle it."

"Well, you did the right thing, Kasey. Trouble is, most young folk haven't been given a good reason to say no to sex and to stay pure. But you take it from this old lady who's been there. It's worth the wait, knowing you have something to bring to that honeymoon that you've shared with no one else on earth, something so special it lights up your marriage for a lifetime." Grams winked knowingly.

"And, Kasey, I can tell you this from experience too. The older you get, the better it gets."

Kasey blushed. "Grams! I can't believe you said that!"

"It's true, and someday I hope you have a marriage like that."

"I hope I can find a man as special as Gramps."

"You will. This Ryan fellow back home sounds pretty nice."

"He's wonderful, Grams. I really do love him. But—"

"But now you've discovered you have some pretty strong feelings for Dusty."

Kasey nodded. "Is something wrong with me for feeling this way? For liking two boys at once?"

"No, Kasey. You sound perfectly normal to me. But it does sound like you've got caught up a little in the physical side of things. That doesn't mean Dusty's a better boyfriend for you than Ryan. It just means there's a powerful attraction there. Actually, there's something else about Dusty I wonder if you've considered."

"What's that, Grams?"

"Is he a Christian? Does he share your faith?"

Kasey pulled at the hem of her nightshirt. "I don't think so. I've tried talking to him about the Lord, but he doesn't say much."

"Well, Kasey, one thing I was warned about when I was young was 'missionary dating.' Thinking you could go with a boy and change him. Make him believe like you believed. Loving someone doesn't necessarily make a person change. And if you're already emotionally involved, it makes things pretty complicated."

"I know what the Bible says, Grams," said Kasey. "We're not supposed to be unequally yoked together with unbelievers, not teamed up with people who don't love the Lord. I feel that way too. But then, when I'm with Dusty—"

"It's hard, isn't it, child? But if you want Dusty to see Jesus in your life, you're going to have to keep things right between you and the Lord."

Kasey sighed. "Right. And that means not getting physically involved. But how can I let Dusty know I still want to be his friend but not his girlfriend?"

Her grandmother smiled. "You'll have to check with the Lord on that one. You keep the lines of communication open, and I think He'll show you the way."

"Thanks, Grams. Now I guess I'd better let you get some sleep." Kasey stood up and smoothed the covers on her grandmother's bed. "Can I get you anything before I go to my room?"

"Maybe a glass of water. And check to see if your granddad's fallen asleep in his chair watching the news on TV."

As Kasey leaned over and kissed her grandmother's forehead, she caught the fragrance of Ivory soap and lilac talc. "I love you, Grams. Thanks for listening."

Her grandmother clasped her hand and said, "Before you go—let's talk about this problem with the merchants in town—them saying you took money from them."

Kasey leaned against the wall, her shoulders sagging. "Like I told you and Gramps earlier, Diana says people suspect me. And she says her dad won't let me work at the Emporium unless Gramps gets rid of Dusty."

Grams looked thoughtful. "Well, I suggest you go talk to Mr. Morley and see what he has to say for himself. Diana has a way of being overly dramatic, even exaggerating things sometimes, so maybe it's not as bad as it seems."

"I hate to face him, Grams. I hate facing everyone in town."

"Don't you feel that way, child. This town isn't made up of a bunch of fools. Most folks know how honest you are. It's just a few bad ones that spoil the bunch."

"If you say so, Grams. I'11 talk to him tomorrow. Good night."

"One last thing, child, then I'll let you head for bed."

Kasey paused in the doorway, her hand on the knob. "Sure, Grams. What?"

"I hope you don't mind me asking, but why aren't you spending more time with the young people at church this summer?"

Kasey smiled wanly. "And less time with Diana and Dusty? Is that what you mean?"

"Maybe. You hardly ever invite the youngsters over from your Sunday school class. Are you afraid of disturbing Gramps and me?"

"No. It's just that most of the kids are busy with their own lives. They work or go to summer school, or both. I see a few of them at church and Sunday school or prayer meeting, and they're friendly enough . . ."

"But—?"

"But they've gone on with their lives, Grams. I don't

97

fit in anymore. It's like they know I'm only here for the summer, so they don't want to make room for me."

"Well, that's a sad state of affairs, if I ever heard tell."

"It's OK, Grams. I only have a few weeks left anyway."

Her grandmother's expression clouded. "I know, child. And I'm going to hate to see you go. You've been such a blessing to your granddad and me all summer. We've loved having you here."

"Me too, Grams."

"Now you go wake your granddad and tell him to get in here to bed. I don't want him spending the night in his easy chair, or he'll be stiff with arthritis in the morning."

Kasey laughed. "I'll try, Grams. But you know what a sound sleeper he is!"

That night Kasey wished she could sleep half as soundly as her grandfather, but her slumber was fitful and punctuated by heart-pounding nightmares. In one vivid, blood-curdling dream, Kasey was attacked by a swarm of blue racers and water moccasins while swimming in the creek. When Kasey stared into the snakes' faces, she recognized Dusty and Mr. Morley and some of the townspeople. In another dream she was back in Springfield with Ryan, and he was kissing her tenderly. But when she drew back and looked at him, it was really Dusty she was kissing, and he began to laugh. Then, amid the laughter, she heard Ryan's voice pleading, "Kasey, don't do this to us. Don't throw our love away on that drifter." But then Dusty broke in, calling urgently, "I need you, Kasey. Help me! No one else will be my friend."

At 3:00 A.M. Kasey woke in a cold sweat. She climbed out of bed and stole to the living room, trying to shake off the dark, lingering shadows of her dreams. She turned the TV on low and curled up in Gramps's easy chair. And that's where she found herself when the sun came up in the morning.

16

After breakfast, Kasey summoned her courage and rode her bicycle into town to the Emporium. She knew she had to face Mr. Morley and get the merchants' suspicions out in the open once and for all. She found Mr. Morley in the back room going over the books. He looked up and gave her a slow, appraising grin. "Well, well, how are you this fine morning, Kasey?"

She nervously clenched and unclenched her clammy hands. "I—I've got to talk to you, Mr. Morley. Do you have a minute?"

"For you, Kasey, I've got all the time you need. Sit down."

She slipped into the chair across from his desk. "I guess you know why I'm here, Mr. Morley."

He leaned his elbows on the desk and put his fingertips together in a little tent formation. "Why don't you tell me, Kasey."

The words tumbled out pell-mell. "Diana told me— she said I can't work here anymore, uh, unless my grandfather fires our hired hand. She says the merchants in town—they think I had something to do with—the robberies."

Mr. Morley's expression remained stoic. "Kasey, you must know I don't really believe you had anything to do with the thefts here in town. I've known you all your life, and I know you wouldn't steal from me."

"But Diana said—"

"I know. Diana heard me say something like that in a moment of anger. You must realize how frustrated all of us are in town with these petty thefts. Obviously someone we all know is the culprit, because we so seldom have strangers in town. And none of the robberies have been what you'd call 'break-ins,' because they all occurred during normal working hours. So you see the dilemma we're in."

Kasey shrugged. "I'm not sure what you're getting at."

"Well, it's the process of elimination. Someone is guilty. But who? Common sense tells us it's more likely to be someone new in town, someone people don't know rather than one of our own. That conclusion has led naturally to your new hired man."

"But Diana said some people are saying I stole the money!"

Mr. Morley sat back in his chair, his fingertips still in their little pyramid. "Yes, a few people have speculated about that possibility, but I think if you pinned them down, they'd have to admit they really don't believe you'd do such a thing."

"But then, what Diana said about you wanting me to quit—"

"Well, Kasey, the problem reverts back again to your hired man. People have this idea that wherever you are, that's where the robberies are more likely to occur, perhaps because of this Jernigan fellow. They wonder if he's not using you somehow to gain access to places he normally wouldn't be. You must admit he's stopped in here a few times to chat with you when you were working."

"Usually just because he had some message from my grandparents. Or he needed to pick up supplies."

"Whatever his reason, he's more likely to appear wherever you are. People have noticed that. So, if Dusty is guilty of the robberies, you, in a sense, become guilty by association. Do you understand?"

"It sounds like convoluted logic to me," murmured Kasey.

"I suppose you're right. Nevertheless—"

Kasey studied Mr. Morley's face. It was like he was wearing a mask of friendliness over something more sinister. "What are trying to tell me, Mr. Morley?"

"Just this, Kasey. I think it might be better for you and for the Emporium if you took a few weeks off and let this whole robbery thing cool down. Come back when people aren't so skittish—"

"But I'll only be here a few more weeks! This is August already. I'll be going back to Springfield in September!"

Mr. Morley was still smiling his pasted-on grin. "Then you'd probably like a little more time for yourself anyway, so maybe this'll work out best all around."

"No, it won't," protested Kasey. "I love working at the Emporium. This was my dad's store. I love this place. I'd never steal from it or let anyone else steal from it! Please, Mr. Morley!"

Mr. Morley stood up. "I'm sorry, Kasey, but as long as that drifter fellow is out at your farm, people are going to be afraid. And you working here will just remind folks what they're afraid of. When you can tell me that man's on his way out of town, then the job's yours again."

Kasey stood up and backed toward the door. "It's not fair, Mr. Morley. I didn't do anything wrong. Dusty didn't do anything wrong."

With almost a breezy air, Mr. Morley escorted her outside the store. "I'm sorry, Kasey," he said, squinting against the sunlight. "My hands are tied. I have a business to run. I can't be sentimental when it comes to protecting my interests." He put his hand on her shoulder. "But this doesn't have to affect our personal relationship. You're welcome at our home to see Diana any time you wish. She considers you a good friend."

"She's my best friend. We've always been best friends," Kasey mumbled. That wasn't what she wanted to say, but no other words came. The impact of Mr. Morley's words had short-circuited Kasey's brain. She felt stunned, out of breath, as if she'd caught a fast ball in the stomach.

Kasey turned away and began walking numbly along the sidewalk toward the bike stand. Inside her chest she could feel the anger rising like a mushroom cloud, like an explosion taking place inside her rib cage. Even as she reached for her bike and climbed onto the seat, rage was running over like molten lava from a volcano.

She was trembling, and she couldn't see, couldn't even think straight. She wanted to get away before she turned around and did something to Mr. Morley or to Mr. Morley's store—slapped him across the face or smashed the plate glass window.

But no. Of course not. She couldn't hurt the store. It had belonged to her mom and dad—the country-style general store they had started and nursed along through years of hard times, the store she loved almost like a person. So many precious memories filled the walls of that wonderful old store.

And now Mr. Morley was sending her away in shame. Tears ran down Kasey's cheeks and blurred her vision.

She pedaled faster and faster. She had to get home before she lost control of the thunder clouds billowing inside her.

As soon as she reached the farm, she dropped her bike on the grass and ran into the house. She hurried to her room before Grams or Gramps could see her. She put on a Dino tape and turned the volume up loud, then buried her face in her pillow and released the downpour. She bawled until her tears were spent and she was caught in a fit of hiccuping.

A sudden knock on the door sent Kasey to the mirror to dry her eyes and repair her smudged mascara. "Just a minute," she called, but the door opened anyway.

"Kasey, it's me. I had to come."

Kasey whirled around. Diana stood in the doorway looking as distressed as Kasey felt. Usually Diana's beauty was flawless, but now she looked pale, almost haggard.

"Kasey, my dad told me what happened. I drove right over. I'm so sorry. I tried to tell you myself, so you wouldn't have to face him. Why did you go there?"

"I guess I'm a glutton for punishment. I had to hear it for myself."

Diana sat down on the bed. "Well, I hope you know, Kasey, no matter what happens, you'll always be my best friend."

Kasey sat down and blew her nose. "Thanks, Diana. You don't know how much I need to hear that now."

The two girls hugged for a moment, then Diana said, "Let me do something for you, Kasey. Something to cheer you up."

"What?"

"Let me stay with your grandmother while you go out and relax."

Kasey managed a smile. "I don't have anywhere to go."

Diana thought a moment. "Well, I remember your grandfather saying he wanted you to help him pick out a new tractor. Why don't you both go, and I'll keep your grandmother company."

Kasey returned to the mirror to finish the repair job on her makeup. "Maybe that would be a good idea. Gramps does need that new tractor desperately, and I did promise to help him shop for it."

"Then it's settled. I'll even fix dinner and have it ready when you get back." Diana gave Kasey another hug. "I know it can't make up for what my dad did, but at least you'll know how I feel."

Kasey felt her spirits perking up already. "It's almost like the old days, isn't is, Diana? When one of us was down, the other one always came up with something to make things better."

Diana flashed a smile. "Friends to the end—right, Kasey?"

17

Gramps was more than a little pleased that Kasey wanted to help him shop for his new tractor. He put on his best plaid shirt Grams had bought for his birthday and a string tie that made him look like a cowboy. Then, with his Levi's and spit 'n' polish boots, he looked for sure like he could have stepped out of an old Roy Rogers movie.

"We'll be driving to Sweetwater and Crest City," he told Grams and Diana. "One of them surely has what I'm looking for."

"You get the best deal you can," said Grams. "Don't buy the first thing you see."

"Now you know me better than that, Emma. I'm not putting any money out today. I'm just shopping around for a good buy."

The shopping trip took all afternoon. There was the drive to Sweetwater, then the drive to Crest City, and a couple hours of browsing at the farm equipment and machinery stores in both towns.

As they shopped, Kasey tried to enter into Gramps's enthusiasm, but she still felt shaken from her conversation with Mr. Morley. While she and Gramps listened to clerks spout the many features and advantages of their tractors, she still heard Mr. Morley's voice in her head: *As long as that drifter fellow is out at your farm, people are going to be afraid.* Even when Gramps bargained with the clerks and haggled over the final price of the tractor of his choice, Kasey wondered how she could resolve her dilemma with Dusty and the townspeople.

All the way home in Gramps's pickup truck, Kasey wavered between pondering her dismal circumstances and listening to her grandfather rave about the tractor he would be buying. As they pulled into the winding driveway to the farmhouse, Gramps exclaimed, "I feel like a little kid at Christmas, Kasey, getting that new tractor! You ever hear tell of such a thing?"

Kasey patted her grandfather's arm. "I think it's great, Gramps. You deserve it. And lots more besides."

"Well, I've worked hard for years to save for it, Kasey. It hasn't been easy squirreling those pennies and dimes away. Your grandma and I have had to do without some things we wanted, but it's worth it. That new tractor will help me mightily with my workload around here."

Grams and Diana had dinner on the table when Kasey and Gramps walked in. "It's about time you two arrived," said Grams, moving slowly toward the door in her walker. "A few minutes more and you'd be eating cold meatloaf and lumpy mashed potatoes."

"Sorry, Emma, but you know how long shopping can take," said Gramps, kissing her cheek. "But dinner looks and smells delicious! I just hope you weren't overdoing it. You know what the doctor says."

"No, I did very little. Diana's responsible for this feast. She worked very hard all afternoon."

Diana set a bowl of creamed cauliflower on the table. "It was my pleasure. I haven't felt so domestic all summer. In fact, if my mother saw me, she'd probably keel over in disbelief."

Kasey turned on the faucet at the kitchen sink and washed her hands. "Did everything go OK while we were gone?"

"Fine," said Diana, joining her at the sink. "Your grandmother had a nice nap while I worked on dinner. I totally enjoyed having the kitchen to myself. It wasn't like at home with my mother constantly peering over my shoulder afraid I'll break a dish or mess something up."

Kasey squeezed Diana's arm. "Thanks for coming. You're a lifesaver. And I'm so glad it went well."

"It did, but—" Diana drew close to Kasey and whispered "—are you aware that your hired man—Dusty—has full run of this house?"

"Well, he's in and out for meals, but—"

"In and out—for sure! He comes and goes as he pleases, like he owns the place. I was amazed. Your grandparents don't even keep the door locked. Dusty comes in without asking and browses in the cupboards and everything. I'd think that would make you nervous, considering all the rumors about him."

Kasey stiffened. "I don't listen to rumors—unlike some people I know," she added, not even caring whether Diana knew she meant her father, Mr. Morley.

Diana shrugged. "OK, I just thought you should know I saw him snooping around here, and when I asked him what he was looking for, he wasn't very pleasant to me."

"That's just Dusty's nature. He didn't mean anything personal."

"Hey," called Gramps. "You gals gonna get over here and sit down so we can say grace and dive into these goodies?"

The girls sat down, and Gramps prayed. Then everyone converged on the food. "Hey, are we supposed to save some of this chow for Dusty?" asked Gramps. "If so, he's gonna have slim pickin's by the time he gets here."

"No," said Diana. "He told me he'd be busy tonight."

"Busy? Doing what? He doesn't have any nighttime chores."

"I don't know," said Diana. "But he seemed kind of—edgy, like he didn't really want to talk about it."

"Well, that's Dusty for you. He has a gloomy streak to him sometimes. He's a hard one to figure."

Kasey thought about telling them what Dusty had told her—about his unhappy family life and his little brother who had died at his father's hands, and how Dusty felt guilty because he wasn't there to save him. But that seemed like private information, and maybe Dusty didn't want anyone else knowing about such personal stuff.

"So, tell us, Tonio, did you find a tractor?" urged Grams.

"I found us a real beauty, Emma. And I got the fellow down in price by promising him a $2,000 down payment in cash. I'm driving back to Sweetwater tomorrow to give him the money and sign the papers."

Grams reached over and took Gramps's hand. "You've waited a long time for that tractor. I'm glad you found what you wanted."

Before they had even finished eating, Diana was up and clearing her place setting. "Please excuse me, Mr. and Mrs. Carlone," she said as she rinsed her plate. "I promised Mom I'd be home before dark. You know how mothers are—worry, worry, worry."

"But you hardly ate anything," said Grams, "and after you worked so hard on this meal."

"I know, but I really don't have much appetite for my own cooking. My mom says she feels that way too. That's why she hardly ever cooks. We eat out a lot, you know."

"Well, you're thin as a rail, Diana," said Grams. "I think you've actually lost weight since I saw you last, so you tell your mother she'd better go back to fixing home-cooked meals."

"I'll tell her," said Diana, going to the sofa and picking up her purse. "I'll see you all later."

Kasey got up and walked her to the door. As Diana stepped out onto the porch, she whispered, "Don't forget what I said. Keep an eye on that hired man of yours. He was roaming around the kitchen the whole time I was in the bedroom helping your grandmother."

Kasey nodded. "I'll mention it to them. He really shouldn't be in the house when they're not here."

"That's what I thought," said Diana, "but he wouldn't listen to me. He's really strange, Kasey. I wouldn't trust him for a minute."

After Diana left, Kasey considered telling her grandparents about Dusty's being in the house without their knowledge, but they were still absorbed in conversation about the tractor, so it didn't seem worth mentioning.

But later that evening something happened that brought back Diana's words with stark, painful clarity. Gramps had retrieved his strongbox from the linen closet and opened it on the kitchen table. Kasey was washing the dishes, with her back to Gramps, when she heard him gasp and moan, "Oh, no!"

She whirled around, fear shooting up her spine. Was Gramps having a heart attack?

He stood with both hands on the table, his stocky frame bent over the strongbox, shaking his head despairingly and uttering, "No, no, no! It can't be!"

"What's wrong, Gramps?" cried Kasey, rushing over and clasping his arm.

He pushed the open strongbox toward her. "Look!"

She peered inside. It was empty. "The money! Gramps? Where is it?"

"It's gone!" He collapsed like a wounded bull into the straight-back chair. "I can't believe it. It's gone! All my money's gone!"

"Maybe Grams put it somewhere else," said Kasey, grasping at straws. "Maybe she put it in her purse or in an envelope for you to take tomorrow."

A mixture of anger and anguish throbbed in her grandfather's voice. "No, Kasey, with her broken hip she can't get in the closet and reach that strongbox. Someone else was in there. Don't you understand? All my cash—my life savings! Somebody stole it!"

18

Reluctantly Kasey told Gramps what Diana had said about Dusty's roaming around the kitchen while she was in the bedroom with Grams.

"But that doesn't mean he stole the money," she added quickly. "The door was unlocked. Maybe someone else got in."

Gramps stared hard at her. There were tears in his eyes. "Do you really believe that, Kasey? Who else could it be?"

Tears stung Kasey's eyes too. "I don't know. I just never thought—"

"Neither did I!" Gramps pounded the table with his fist, so hard the empty strongbox bounced. "I was an old fool, believing in that boy when the whole town knew better. But I was a softy, wanting to give him a chance, give him the benefit of a doubt. Now look where it got me."

"But maybe he can explain, Gramps. Maybe if we talked to him—"

"We'll talk to him, all right." Her grandfather pivoted and stalked through the door, letting the screen slam behind him.

Kasey threw open the door and ran after him. "Wait, Gramps! I'm coming with you!"

The night air was heavy with the kind of humidity that gathered just before a storm. Kasey caught the smell of rain in her nostrils as she darted through the grass toward the bunkhouse. Usually she loved that smell, but tonight it seemed to linger with a dark foreboding. She shivered as the dampness closed around her, blending with the perspiration on her forehead.

"Dusty? Dusty Jernigan! You in there?" Gramps shouted as he hammered on the bunkhouse door.

"There's no light," said Kasey. "Maybe he's already asleep."

"Then I'll knock loud enough to wake the dead. Dusty! Open up! I wanna talk to you!"

"Maybe it's unlocked," said Kasey.

Gramps tried the door. It was unlocked. "I don't usually violate someone's privacy, but at a time like this—" He opened the door and stepped inside, flipping the light switch. Kasey followed gingerly, a step behind. "Dusty? You here?"

No answer.

They looked around. "No sign of him, Kasey."

"Where would he be this time of night?" she asked.

"Where do you think? If he took my money, he's not gonna hang around waiting for me to come ask for it back."

"You mean he's gone? For good?" Kasey asked incredulously.

"Looks that way." Her grandfather threw open the closet door and pulled out several dresser drawers. "His stuff's still here, what little he had. A few clothes. Not much."

"Then maybe he didn't run away. Maybe he's still here."

Gramps bent down and picked something up off the floor. "Look at this, Kasey."

"What is it?"

He held out a pack of dollar bills with a rubber band around them. "My money, Kasey," he said, his voice raw with anguish. "That's how I kept them in the strongbox —ten ones with a rubber band, ten fives, ten tens, and so on. He must have dropped this packet of ones accidently. Looks like it's all that's left of my money."

Kasey couldn't keep a sob from rising in her throat. "I'm so sorry, Gramps. You wanted to let Dusty go, and I insisted he stay."

"It's not your fault, Kasey, my girl. I wanted to believe in him too. Nothing wrong with believing in something, except when it lets you down. Looks like Dusty let us down."

They walked back to the house in silence. It was sprinkling lightly now. The raindrops mingled with Kasey's tears. As they climbed the porch steps, she asked, "What are you going to do, Gramps? Are you going to tell Grams?"

"Not yet, if I don't have to. She was asleep when I opened the strongbox. Might as well let her get a good night's rest."

When they entered the kitchen, her grandfather went straight to the phone and dialed. "Hello, police? That you, Jed? Yeah, this is Tonio Carlone. Got me a problem out here. Someone stole my life savings right out from under my nose." Gramps's voice grew gravelly and uneven. "Yeah, I think it was him. Sure, I know, everyone warned me. OK, Jed, so I was a jackass to trust the boy. Throwing the blame around won't bring back my money. Can you send a man out? The boy doesn't have a car—unless he stole one. He's probably out there somewhere hitchhiking. I figure maybe we can track him down and get back my money. Great. See you shortly."

Gramps hung up the phone and turned to Kasey. "Jed Connors, the deputy sheriff, is on his way over. We're going out looking for Dusty. Maybe it's not too late, Kasey."

She gave her grandfather a big bear hug. "I hope not, Gramps."

Her grandfather had just put on his raincoat, boots, and old leather cowboy hat when they heard the squad car pull up in the driveway. Gramps didn't wait for Jed to come in. As he strode out the door, he told Kasey, "You stay here with Grams. I'm gonna ride along with Jed to look for Dusty. We'll try the main roads first."

"Be careful, Gramps!" she called, adding softly, "Please don't let anyone hurt Dusty."

Gramps paused on the porch and looked back at her. "Don't worry, Kasey, my girl. I don't want to hurt the boy. I just want my money back."

"But if there's trouble—if he resists—someone could get hurt."

"We'll do our best, Kasey." Gramps went outside, and Kasey could hear him talking with the deputy. Then she heard the roar of the engine as the police car squealed around the driveway and sped back down the road away from the farmhouse.

Suddenly, the house rang with an ominous silence. Kasey sat down on the sofa and hugged her arms against her chest. She couldn't remember when she had felt so alone. The pain swelled inside her like a balloon pressing on her heart. An actual physical pressure.

How she ached for Dusty, for Gramps, for herself. *Dear Lord, how could things have gone so wrong? How could Gramps and I have been so wrong about Dusty? How can things ever be right again?*

Kasey stood up and paced the floor. Her mind raced. She wondered how long it would take for them to find Dusty? Would he give up without a fight and give back the money? Or would he behave like a trapped animal and do something terrible and impulsive? Would he get hurt? God forbid, would Gramps get hurt? No, Jed was there. He was a policeman, a deputy sheriff. He would see that no one got hurt, wouldn't he? *Wouldn't he?*

Kasey realized she was trembling. Her stomach was in knots. If only she had someone to talk to, someone to help calm her nerves. She thought about waking Grams, then immediately dismissed the idea. Her grandmother had been through enough with her broken hip. Kasey couldn't dump all this on her too. Like Gramps said, it was better if they waited until morning. Maybe by then everything would be back to normal.

Oh, God, please let it be, she prayed silently. *Please let everything be OK again!*

Then Kasey thought of Diana. Surely Diana would want to help. What were best friends for, if not to be together in times of trouble? And this was the worst trouble Kasey had ever known—her grandparents' life savings gone, her grandfather possibly in danger, the boy she cared for obviously a thief!

Kasey ran to the phone and dialed her friend. Drumming her fingers on the table, she counted the rings, then sighed with relief when she heard Diana's voice. The words tumbled from Kasey's mouth, jumbled and confused, but filled with urgency, all about Dusty and the theft. Out of breath, Kasey finished with, "Please, come right over, Diana. I need you!"

Diana's voice sounded wary, concerned. "Are you OK, Kasey? Are you sure you're OK?"

"Yes, but I don't want to be here alone. Please, Diana, I can't stand waiting, not knowing what's happening. Please come as soon as you can."

"I'll be there, Kasey. Give me a few minutes to get dressed and tell Mom where I'm going. You just hold on till I get there. It'll be OK. I promise."

Kasey felt better as she hung up the receiver. Diana would be here, and they could sit and talk and maybe even pray together. Everything would be all right. Everything was always cheerier when Diana was around.

Kasey dried her eyes and blew her nose. She went to the bathroom and ran a comb through her hair and washed the mascara from under her eyes. She powdered her nose and cleaned her glasses. She felt much better, almost optimistic. Somehow, the Lord would make everything OK. He always came through in a crisis. She just had to trust Him.

Suddenly she heard a noise outside, then footsteps on the porch and the screen door slamming as someone entered the house. Who could it possibly be? It was too soon for Diana to arrive, and surely Gramps and Jed wouldn't be back yet. Why hadn't she made sure the door was locked after Gramps left?

An undercurrent of excitement and anxiety raised goose bumps on Kasey's arms as she ran to the living room. As she stared through the golden glow of lamplight toward the door, a wave of fear and shock rippled over her. Dusty stood in the doorway, dripping wet, his dark hair tousled by wind and rain.

Kasey met his stormy gaze and gasped. "D-Dusty, what are you doing here?"

19

"Man, it's raining cats and dogs out there!" Dusty exclaimed, shaking water from his hair. He moved toward Kasey, and she took a quick step backward. "What is it, Kasey?" he asked. "What's wrong?"

She struggled to find the words, any words. "Where —where were you?"

"In the rain. Can't you tell?" He chuckled as if he'd made a joke.

"But where?" she persisted.

"Down at the creek." He went to the kitchen and grabbed a towel from the counter and mopped his face. She followed what she considered a safe distance behind.

"The creek? You were at the creek?"

"Yeah. Stupid, wasn't it? I should have known it was going to rain buckets. I could smell it in the air."

"Why would you go to the creek?" she asked urgently. It was a dumb question. What did it matter why he went to the creek? The important question was, Why did he steal from her grandfather? But, with her heart hammering with fear, how could she confront him with that question?

"I like going to the creek. You know that," he was saying, apparently answering her question. "Remember the day we went? That was one of the best days of my life. I told you then, I go there a lot and just sit and think. It's the most peaceful spot on earth."

"Then you haven't seen my grandfather?" she asked. Why hadn't she just said "Gramps"? "Grandfather" sounded so formal. She didn't want to make Dusty suspicious. Then again, she had to have answers.

"No, I haven't seen your grandfather," said Dusty. "You mean he's out somewhere in weather like this?"

"Yes. He's out looking for you."

"But his truck's right outside, Kasey. He couldn't be looking for me."

Kasey was digging herself into a hole, and she didn't know how to stop. "Gramps is with Jed Connors, the deputy sheriff. They're both looking for you, Dusty!"

He put down the towel and came over to her, reaching out his hand to touch her face. She darted back around the kitchen table.

"What's going on, Kasey?" he asked solemnly. "You look like you've seen a ghost."

"I have! It's you, Dusty," she agonized. "Why did you come back?"

He tried approaching her again, more slowly now. "Tell me what's going on, Kasey. Why are you so upset? What's wrong?"

She stifled a sob. "How can you ask me that? You know what's wrong!"

"No, I don't know. Everything was fine when I went down to the creek a couple hours ago. Now I come back and you're acting like something terrible happened. Is it your grandmother? Is she ill?"

"No, of course not." Kasey couldn't bear any more of this charade. "It's you, Dusty. We all know. You don't have to pretend anymore."

He pulled a straight-back chair out from the table and sat down. "This is weird, Kasey. Really weird. Why don't you sit down and tell me what's on your mind."

She stood at the opposite end of the table, gripping the back of a chair. She felt as if her knees would buckle. "Please give back the money," she blurted. "Please don't hurt Gramps like this!"

Dusty stared open-mouthed at her. "Hurt Gramps? Are you kidding? I love that old man."

The words tore from her throat. "Then why did you take his money?"

"Take what money?" Dusty demanded. "What are you talking about, Kasey?"

"Gramps's savings. He was going to buy a tractor tomorrow. Now it's gone!"

"You're saying the money he saved for the tractor is missing?"

"You know it is!" cried Kasey. "You took it!"

Dusty jumped up, slamming his chair backward so that it clattered on the floor. "Me? You think I took the money?"

Kasey was crying now. "Why did you do it, Dusty? I cared so much about you. I thought you cared too."

He came over and pulled her against him and pressed her head against his chest. "This is some crazy mistake, Kasey. You gotta start from the beginning and tell me what happened."

For one crazy moment she longed for his comforting touch, but just as quickly, terror replaced the yearning. How did she think she could trust a man who was a liar and a thief? What else might he do? If he were cornered, would he react like a wild animal and harm her and her grandmother? She wriggled out of his grasp and backed away from him.

"Kasey? Did you hear me?" he demanded. "Tell me what's going on. What about your grandfather's savings?"

She tried to find her voice. "You know. The money was in the strongbox. In the linen closet. You saw him put it there. You were here. I remember. You're the only one who could have taken it."

"You really believe that, Kasey? That I'd steal from your grandfather?"

"Who else?" she whimpered, moving slowly backward into the living room.

He followed her, his expression darkening, his gaze riveting. "You think I'm a thief? As close as we've been? A common thief?"

"I didn't want to believe it—"

"But you do!"

"You can't deny it, Dusty. We found proof—some of the money in the bunkhouse!"

"Well, I never put it there!" he roared. "I never took a penny of your grandfather's money!"

Kasey backed into the sofa and sat down. She couldn't keep back her sobs. They shuddered through her chest as she tried to speak. "If you'd just—bring the money back, Gramps would—forgive you. He—he'd help you, Dusty. I'd help you too. We'd do everything we could."

He bent down on one knee beside the sofa and looked her directly in the eye. "Kasey, listen to me." He took her hand and pressed it against his chest. His shirt was wet, his hand bone-cold and trembling. "Kasey, I'm telling you the truth. I never took that money. I didn't do it. Please say you believe me."

She ached with torment for him, but it wasn't enough. "I-I'm sorry, Dusty. I can't!"

He stood up and ran his fingers through his tangled hair. "OK. So you believe I came in here and got in the strongbox and helped myself to your grandfather's savings—right?"

She nodded.

"Then what am I doing here talking to you? How come I'm not a hundred miles from here by now?"

"I—I don't know."

"You don't know—but you still think I'm guilty, right?"

She looked up desolately at him. "I'm sorry, Dusty." But why was *she* sorry? *He* was the guilty one. "If you'd just tell the truth, Dusty, everything could be worked out."

Anger edged his voice now. "The truth is, I'm outa here." He stalked toward the door.

Kasey jumped up and started after him. "Where are you going?"

He gripped the doorknob and looked back at her. "I'm going to the bunkhouse for my stuff. Then, I hit the road."

"Where?"

"Anywhere but here."

"Tell me!"

"I'll hitch a ride somewhere. Maybe to the end of the earth, who knows?"

"But you can't run away, Dusty. You'll never stop running."

"There's nothing for me here, Kasey." His voice cracked, and he rubbed his jaw as if he thought it might keep the emotion back. "I thought you were my friend, Kasey, but I was wrong."

"No, Dusty, you weren't wrong!"

"Really? Well, listen good. No one ever accepted me for myself, Kasey. I really thought you had, but I was wrong about that too." He drew in a deep breath. "You know, it's funny. I felt closer to you this summer than I've ever felt to anyone. I thought you were an angel from heaven. But you're not. You're like everyone else."

She was weeping again. "I'm not, Dusty. I believed in you."

"Yeah, but not enough, right? After all we shared together, if you can't stand by me, what chance do I have? I might as well give up."

She approached him and cautiously reached out her hand. "Don't say that, please. I want to be your friend, but—"

He scowled, his lip curling in a sneer. "I know. You don't wanna be the friend of a *thief*." He spit out the word, then threw open the door and stepped onto the porch. "You gave me this line about how much you and God cared about me, Kasey. I almost believed it. Man, you don't know how I wanted to believe it!" He snapped his fingers in the air. "Well, so much for God's love and all that rot!"

Before she could utter a reply, he took the porch steps two at a time and disappeared into the blinding downpour.

20

Kasey shut the door against the drenching rain and pressed her back against the frame, weeping. Her mind whirled with unanswered questions. How could things have gone so wrong? How could she have been so fooled by Dusty's charm? How could he have betrayed her and her grandparents when they had taken him in like a member of the family?

And the hardest question of all: Why did Kasey still care so deeply for Dusty after all he had done to hurt her?

She sat down on the sofa in the living room and rocked back and forth, hugging her arms against her chest. What should she do now? Gramps and Jed were still out looking for Dusty, and Dusty was in the bunkhouse packing, and Gramps's money was still missing. Should she telephone the police and tell them Dusty was here? They could radio the squad car and tell Jed to return to the farm.

But the thought of Dusty leaving the bunkhouse and running smack into the police sent a wave of revulsion through Kasey. She couldn't be instrumental in his capture. She couldn't bear to see him carted off to jail. But what about Gramps's money? What if Dusty left with it now? Gramps would never be able to afford his new tractor. He would have to begin saving all over again.

Kasey reached for the telephone, then hesitated. "Oh, dear Lord, what should I do? Should I call the police, or—?"

Before she could finish her sentence, there was a knock on the door. She hurried over and peered out the little window. It was Diana.

"Come in," she cried, opening the door to her friend.

"I'm soaked," Diana moaned, pulling off a rain hat and shaking her long blonde curls. "I'm sorry I took so long. My folks weren't going to let me out in this weather. I really had to talk fast. Even then, they made me promise to drive under the speed limit. Those roads are treacherous. And the back roads are already little rivers."

Kasey took Diana's raincoat and hung it on the hat rack by the door. "Do you want some hot chocolate? It'll just take a minute—"

Diana nodded. "Looks like you could use some too."

"I could." They went to the kitchen, and Diana sat at the table while Kasey got out a pan and poured in two cups of milk. She put it on the stove, then reached into the refrigerator for the chocolate syrup. Through the window, she could see flashes of lightning that lit up the outside like daylight. Each was followed by a drumroll of thunder that rumbled like cannon fire in the distance.

Kasey peered out the window toward the bunkhouse. In the lightning flashes, she thought she saw Dusty's shadowy form moving toward the driveway. "Oh, no," she uttered under her breath.

Diana got up and joined her at the window. "What is it? What did you see?"

"Look."

In the next lightning flash, Diana saw it too—a fleeting figure in the rain running toward the road. "Dusty?" she exclaimed.

"He was here," said Kasey. "He denied the robbery. He got mad and said he was leaving."

"Aren't you going to stop him?"

"How?"

"Call the police."

"I was going to, just before you got here—"

"Well, let's do it." Diana went to the phone and dialed. As Kasey distractedly stirred the hot chocolate, she listened to Diana rehash the events of the robbery. "Mr. Carlone and the sheriff are out looking for Dusty now, but you must tell them he came back to the farmhouse. Yes, he's just leaving again. We saw him. What do you mean —who? Do I have to spell it out for you? I'm talking about the man who stole Mr. Carlone's money out of the strongbox in his linen closet. What? All right, thank you. Yes, of course, we'll be careful."

Diana hung up and returned to the table. "I can't believe that lady. She couldn't get a thing straight. How do they ever capture criminals with people like that taking their calls?"

Kasey set two cups of hot chocolate on the table. "What did she say?"

"She said she'd tell the sheriff to head back here."

Kasey sipped her drink, but it was too hot. Where she had burned her tongue, it felt raw. At least she hadn't made the call that would bring the police back after Dusty. Small comfort!

"Don't worry, Kasey, they'll get him," said Diana. "All we have to do is sit and wait."

Kasey sighed. Why did she feel so miserable at that prospect? After a moment, she said, "I should go check on

125

Grams. She's slept through this whole thing. I'd better make sure she's OK."

Kasey was back a minute later. "It's a good thing I checked. Grams was stirring. She told me to tell Gramps to turn off the TV and come to bed. She thinks all the commotion around here was his TV playing too loud."

"Did you tell her?"

"No. I couldn't. She was half asleep anyway. I'll let Gramps tell her when he gets home." Kasey sank back in her chair and drank her hot chocolate. It was almost too cool now, but it didn't matter. She really wasn't thirsty. All she could think about was Dusty. Dusty stealing Gramps's money. Dusty running away and not even caring that he was hurting them. Dusty—

. . . *He stole the money out of the strongbox in the linen closet. . .*

Who had said that? Diana, when she was talking with the police. But there was something strange about that, something not quite right. What was it? It had bothered Kasey the moment she heard Diana say the words, but why?

Then it struck her with a thud in the pit of her stomach. Kasey had never mentioned where the money was. How did Diana know?

Kasey looked up with a quizzical glance.

Diana met her gaze and smiled. "What is it, Kasey? What are you thinking?"

"I—I was just wondering—"

"What?"

"How you knew where the money was. I never told you."

"Sure you did. When you telephoned me."

"No. I know I didn't. All I said was that Gramps had been robbed. I never told you where he kept his money."

126

"Get real, Kasey. It was common knowledge. I've been here and seen your grandfather with his strongbox out. I've seen him put money in it. Where else would it have been?"

"You knew where Gramps kept his money?"

"Sure. He never tried to hide it."

Kasey mulled over this new information. "For some reason, I thought Dusty was the only one outside our family who knew where Gramps kept his savings."

Irritation crept into Diana's voice. "For heaven's sake, what difference does it make, Kasey?"

Kasey turned the warm cup between her palms. "None, I guess, except—except that means you could have taken the money just as easily as Dusty. You were here today, Diana. You had as much opportunity as he did."

Diana's face flushed with indignation. She bristled and lifted her chin. "I can't believe I'm hearing this from my best friend."

Kasey shook her head slowly. "I'm not accusing you, Diana. It's just that I—I feel so awful about Dusty. I was hoping he'd get to know Jesus like you and I do, but now, after all this, I don't think it'll ever happen."

"You don't know that."

"No, but if there's even the slightest chance he didn't take the money—well, he'd never forgive me for blaming him. And I don't think he'd ever be open to hearing about God again."

Diana stirred her hot chocolate methodically. She kept her eyes on the cup, while her mouth settled into a little pout. "All this fuss over a couple thousand dollars," she muttered.

Kasey looked at her. After a moment, Diana looked up and met her gaze, then flinched ever so slightly. The silence hung between them like a heavy curtain. At last, Kasey said quietly, "I never told you how much was stolen."

Diana shrugged. "I know."

The thunder rolled in the distance, and the lightning flashed in the windows. Diana and Kasey remained motionless and silent for what seemed an eternity. Then Kasey whispered, "Why did you do it, Diana?"

Diana pushed her cup away and propped her elbows on the table. She covered her face with her hands so that Kasey couldn't see her eyes. She sat that way for several moments. Finally she said, "I had to."

Kasey raised her voice. "You had to?"

Diana nodded. She looked at Kasey. Her eyes were wet. Something in the usually polished veneer of her face had broken. Her lower lip was trembling. "I—I needed the money."

"You—you needed the money? You must be kidding. Your folks are rich. You have everything you want!"

"No, I don't." In a small, childlike voice, she said, "I need something they won't give me."

Kasey couldn't stifle the confusion and disbelief sweeping over her. "What? You have a new car, beautiful clothes, money to burn. What else could you possibly need?"

A long pause, then: "Crack."

Kasey thought she hadn't heard right. "What did you say?"

Diana's voice was a monotone. "Crack. You know. Crack cocaine."

Kasey was stunned. This conversation couldn't be happening. It couldn't possibly be real. "Are you saying —are you telling me you're on—cocaine?"

Diana's nose was running. She wiped it with the back of her hand. "I—I tried quitting, going cold turkey a while ago. I went almost a month once, but then I got high again, and that was it. Now—now I don't even try to stop anymore. I just gotta have it, Kasey."

"But how? Where do you get it? Who got you started?"

Diana heaved a bleak sigh. "Sonja. Her friends. It happened the first time I went to Bloomington. Last October. They said, 'Try it just once.' So I did. Crack. It was better than sex." She met Kasey's startled gaze. "Yeah, sex. I tried that too."

Kasey sat back in her chair and stared hard at the girl who had been her best friend since grade school. Was this the same person she had thought she knew better than anyone else in the world? Had they ever really known each other? Diana Morley was suddenly a stranger, worse than a stranger. At least with a stranger there was no emotion invested, no history shared, no potential of wounding one another.

"I don't know what to say," Kasey murmured. "Maybe you better tell me everything. You know. About taking my grandfather's money."

Diana bit her lip and admitted reluctantly, "It wasn't just your grandfather, Kasey."

Now, suddenly, another truth was dawning. "You mean, the money stolen from the merchants in town— from your own father's store—?"

Diana began to weep. "You gotta believe me, Kasey. I never meant to hurt anyone. I never wanted to steal. I swear to you, I hated myself. Every time it happened, I swore I'd never do it again. But the dealers Sonja buys from—they kept raising their prices. Middleton and Bloomington aren't like New York or L.A., with a dealer on every corner. I had to pay what they asked."

She paused, her breathing ragged. "I owed them so much, Kasey, they were starting to make threats. I couldn't ask my dad for any more money. He was getting suspicious. I didn't know what else to do. I was so scared. You don't know what it's like, Kasey, needing something so bad your skin crawls and your stomach turns inside out with the craving. Nothing else matters except getting high again. You'd rather be dead than go without it. You've got to understand what it's like—how bad it can get. That's why I took the money."

Kasey shook her head, dumbfounded. "So you stole from people who are your friends, people you've known all your life? You robbed your own father and made it look like Dusty did it? You let Dusty take the blame?"

"I had to." Diana sobbed disconsolately. Her mascara was smudged and making black rivulets down her cheeks. She wiped her eyes with her fingertips, smearing her makeup even more. Kasey had never seen her look more pathetic. "Don't you see, Kasey? Dusty was a stranger. People were naturally suspicious. It was easy to help myself to the cash register on days he stopped in the store."

Diana gulped several tremulous breaths, rubbing her cheek distractedly. She was a little calmer now. "And then I started hitting other stores, Kasey, ones I noticed Dusty had been in. Everyone knew me. They didn't think anything of me popping in for a visit. I couldn't believe how incredibly easy it was."

Kasey swayed in her chair. "This is totally unreal, Diana. Totally. I think I'm going to be sick."

"I'm so sorry. Please don't hate me, Kasey." Diana reached out and clasped Kasey's hand. "I never would have done it, believe me. But Sonja was putting pressure on me for the money I owed her. The dealers were pressuring her. Remember the night you went with me to Bloomington? That's when I knew I had to do something. I had to get the money somehow." She was breathing harder again, speaking faster and faster. "Then I got this idea, Kasey. I'd just take a little money here and there. Not enough to make any difference or to make anyone really mad. I figured nobody would get hurt if I made it look like Dusty was guilty. After all, he's just a drifter. You understand, don't you, Kasey? Maybe he's already in trouble with the law. I figured if the police came after him, he'd run and no one would be the wiser."

"Dusty—run?" Kasey pushed back her chair and stood up. "Oh, no. I almost forgot. He's running right now. He thinks I believe he's guilty. I've got to stop him!"

Diana stood up too. "What are you talking about, Kasey?"

She ran to the door and grabbed Diana's raincoat. "I've got to find him, Diana. If I don't tell him I believe in him, he'll never stop running. He'll never trust anyone, not even God."

Diana stepped between Kasey and the door. "You can't go out in a thunderstorm like this. You'll never find him. He's long gone."

Kasey hesitated. "You're right. I can't go out walking in this downpour. I've got to drive."

"Drive? Drive what?"

Kasey looked questioningly at her.

"Oh, no, not my car you don't!"

Kasey turned and started for her grandparents' bedroom. "OK, then I'll take Gramps's truck."

Diana followed right behind her. "You can't. You told me yourself you hate driving that truck. Besides, you don't even know how to drive a straight-stick, do you?"

"I'll figure it out." Kasey was back in a moment with the keys to her grandfather's pickup. "You stay here with my grandmother, Diana. And if my grandfather gets back with Jed, you tell them the whole story. The truth, Diana! And you better pray that I come back with Dusty!"

21

Kasey forged out into the slanting rain, her head lowered against the raging gusts of wind. With raindrops pelting her face like machine gun fire, she slogged through the soggy earth to her grandfather's pickup, fumbled with the lock, and climbed inside.

At least in the cab of the truck she had protection from the elements. The rain could swirl and the lightning flash around her, but she was safe in this damp little cubicle that smelled faintly of rubber and upholstery and gasoline. Yes, she was safe in Gramps's truck—until she tried to drive it. Why hadn't she let her grandfather show her how to drive a stick shift when she first got her license? *Because you moved away from Middleton, silly,* she chided herself.

Taking a deep breath, she turned the key in the ignition. The engine turned over and died. She tried again. It died again. She shook her head despairingly. The engine must be wet. Maybe this was as far as she would get in her mission of mercy.

"Please, Lord, let me find Dusty before he's gone forever," she whispered. Her voice seemed too loud, filling the little cab. She tried the engine again. This time it coughed and sputtered. Again. Ah, praise the Lord, it was purring like a kitten!

She turned on the headlights and windshield wipers, then shifted into gear the way she had seen Gramps do it. And she was on her way! She drove down the driveway —what she believed to be the driveway in this torrential downpour—and turned onto the road. She sat forward, her entire body tense as a tightrope walker on a highwire. Peering through the glass at the highway ahead, she could see only a few yards, and even her limited visibility was distorted by the swirls of rain drumming patterns against the windshield.

Her hands were knuckle-white on the steering wheel, and her stomach churned with waves of dread and urgency. She had to find Dusty. Simply had to. His life was in her hands. Dusty knew how that felt—to have someone's life in your hands and have it snatched away when maybe you could have done something to stop it. He hadn't been there when his little brother was beaten; he wasn't there to defend him, to take the beating himself. And his brother had died. It was a burden of guilt Dusty would carry all his life.

Kasey wondered if she'd end up carrying such a burden herself. In years to come, would she look back on this night as the time she hadn't been there for someone—for Dusty? Would she regret this night for the rest of her life because she wasn't able to find him and bring him home and convince him somebody cared? She cared. God cared. But would Dusty ever know that now?

Only if she found him!

She pressed her foot on the accelerator and felt the tires wheeze and spin on the flooded pavement. *Be careful,*

Kasey. Too much speed and you'll go sliding all over the highway. She peered through the windshield, trying to focus her gaze on the side of the road. But the wipers swooshed back and forth, sending streams of water across her line of vision. What if she drove right by Dusty without even seeing him? What if he had taken another road? He would probably head for the main highway where he could hitch a ride. That's where she would go too.

She pressed on through the deluge with dogged determination, flinching when the lightning snaked across the sky or split the heavens with jagged, white-hot bolts. When the thunder rumbled around her like the bass section of some heavenly orchestra, she sang hymns to herself and talked out loud to God. "Dear Jesus, You're my best Friend in all the world. Please don't let me be afraid. Help me to find Dusty. Let him know how much You love him."

Even as she said the words, she spotted a ghostly form ahead, loping along the roadside. It had to be Dusty. Who else would be out on a night like this? She slowed down and laid her hand on the horn. The figure looked around. Yes, it was Dusty! She braked beside him, leaned over, and pushed open the door. "Get in," she shouted over the drumming rain.

He gripped the door and stared in at her. He was drenched, his hair plastered against his head like little black snakes, the water running in streams down his face and off his sturdy chin. "Go home, Kasey," he shouted rawly. "I'm no good for you. Just go home!"

"No, Dusty," she shouted back. "Get in. You're not guilty. I know you didn't steal the money!"

He cupped his hand to his ear. "Can't hear you! Go home!" He slammed the door, stepped back away from the truck, and waved her on.

"Dusty, no! Stop!" she screamed. "Come back!"

He pivoted and kept walking, his head down, his lanky legs taking long strides. Kasey followed slowly behind him, her hand on the horn. Whenever a car passed, swerving impatiently around Kasey because she was going too slow, Dusty ran alongside the vehicle, waving his hand, thumbing a ride. After two or three cars had gone by, a van stopped and picked him up.

"No, Dusty, wait!" Kasey cried as the van picked up speed and disappeared into the drizzle. She pressed her foot on the gas and lurched forward. She was driving too fast for weather like this, but if she lost that van, then Dusty was gone for good. Somehow she had to reach him and make him realize she had been wrong about him. She had to tell him he still had a home with her grandparents and that there were people who cared about him. Including Kasey Carlone.

Her headlights carved only a meager path through the torrent. She kept her eyes fastened on the outside white line, but too often it was obliterated by the squall. If only it would stop raining long enough for her to see where she was going! And if only she were accustomed to driving Gramps's truck and handling a stick shift!

She realized suddenly that she could no longer see the lights of the van ahead of her. Had it turned off somewhere? How could it be? She had come so close to taking Dusty back home. Now, he might be lost to her forever. And lost to the Lord as well!

As Kasey accelerated, she felt the heavy tires grind and miss on the slick pavement. She gripped the wheel and struggled for control, but the truck was already sliding, veering toward the oncoming lane. All her senses jumped to attention. With panic shooting like ice through her veins, she turned the steering wheel hard to the left. A failed gesture. The truck spun out of control. She lost sight of the white line as the pickup shot off the flooded highway like a missile in flight.

Suddenly everything was in chaos, jumbled and spinning. Like a roller-coaster off its tracks, the truck careened downward toward a ravine, and Kasey with it, her body taut against the restraints of her seat belt. Sky and trees and gales of rain flashed across the windshield as she plummeted pell-mell, like Alice in Wonderland falling down the White Rabbit's hole. Then the grotesque limbs of a monstrous oak rose up in her path with a sudden, shattering explosion of sound—metal ripping and collapsing like a paper accordion, accompanied by a terrifying blackness that blotted out Kasey's world. When the grisly echo of impact had died, only the steady rat-a-tat of pattering rain broke the tomblike silence of the night.

22

Light. White and blinding, pressing on her eyes. And pain. Searing through her skull. Kasey strained to open her eyes, but the glaring light made her blink. Gradually she forced her lids open and tried to focus her gaze. The world was swimming in a haze of fuzzy pastels; everything blurred and shrank away, then popped back sharp and crystal clear, but with surreal proportions. She was in a room. People were hovering over her. But their faces were indistinct, distorted, like Silly Putty. Like reflections in a fun house mirror.

"Kasey, do you hear me? Nod if you hear me. Kasey, can you tell me your name? What's your name, dear?"

It seemed like a stupid question. Whoever was speaking was already calling her Kasey. When he repeated the question, she dutifully answered, "Kasey. Kasey Carlone."

"Terrific, Kasey. You're doing super. Keep it up."

Super? For knowing her name? What kind of game was this?

She could see him now. The haze was clearing. A stranger in white. A doctor. Her mind was coming into focus along with her vision. "Where am I?" she asked.

"The hospital, Kasey. You had an accident. Do you remember?"

Yes, it was coming back in painful fragments, shards of memory that triggered fresh anguish and regret: the robbery, Dusty running, Diana confessing, Kasey braving the downpour to look for Dusty, then the truck going out of control, over the embankment into the tree.

The doctor was speaking. "How are you feeling, Kasey?"

How did he think she was feeling? Like she was run over by a truck! "I—I hurt," she murmured.

"Where, Kasey?"

"Everywhere."

He smiled and took her hand. "But you're going to be fine. You'll have a headache for a day or two, and you've got some bruises, but you were a very lucky girl."

"Lucky?"

"Yes. You could have been killed if you weren't wearing your seat belt. God was certainly watching over you."

Kasey knew that was true. She must have kept her guardian angel working overtime during that storm. But what about Dusty? She hadn't been able to stop him. Now she would never see him again.

"There's someone waiting to see you, Kasey," said the doctor.

For an instant her hopes soared, but then she spotted her grandfather approaching the bedside. Not Dusty. Gramps. But that was OK. She smiled up at him.

He leaned over and kissed her forehead. "Hi, Kasey, my girl. Am I glad to see you."

"Hi, Gramps, she murmured bleakly. "Are you and Grams OK?"

"We're fine, though your grandma was mad as a hornet when she found out all that was going on while she slept. She wonders why you didn't wake her."

"I couldn't, Gramps. I didn't want to upset her." Kasey drew in a deep breath. It made her chest hurt. "I'm sorry about your truck, Gramps. Is it totaled?"

"Don't you worry, child. I got good insurance. I'll have me a new truck. I'm just mighty glad you're OK, because I couldn't get me a new granddaughter."

She felt tears well up in her eyes. "I really messed things up, Gramps. I just wanted to help, but I made everything worse."

"Not true, not true. Maybe because of you, things are finally going to be made right around here."

Kasey looked up quizzically at him. "But how?"

He pulled over a chair and sat down beside her. "Well, for starters, Diana Morley has confessed. Told the police she took my money—and committed all the robberies the town's been blaming on Dusty. But then I guess she already told you the whole story."

"Yes, Gramps. Did she tell you about—uh—taking cocaine?"

"That she did. She's a distraught young lady, Kasey."

"Did the police—arrest her?"

"They booked her, then released her into her parents' custody. Needless to say, the Morleys are more than a little upset by all that's happened." Gramps cleared his throat. Kasey could tell that he was struggling with his own deep emotions. "Tell you what I did, Kasey. I telephoned Pastor Jensen, and he went over and talked with the Morleys. They're all going to work together to get Diana into a drug rehabilitation program. She was so upset about your accident, Kasey, she said she'd do anything to kick the habit."

"I'm glad to hear that," Kasey mumbled. But she couldn't help thinking that it was too bad all this hadn't happened soon enough to keep Dusty from running away.

Gramps reached over and patted her hand. "And listen to this, Kasey. Your folks are on their way here right now. Driving up from Springfield. Should be here any time."

"I guess I really scared them, huh?"

"You scared us all, girl. Thank God, you're all right —though no thanks to yourself. It was a fool thing to do, taking my truck out in that blinding rainstorm."

"I know, Gramps, but I had to find Dusty. I had to tell him I knew he wasn't guilty, that I believed in him." Her voice broke. "But it's too late, Gramps. I couldn't stop him. And now I'll probably never see him again."

A smile flickered on her grandfather's lips. "Oh, I suspect you'll see Dusty again soon."

Kasey tried to raise her head. "How, Gramps? Tell me!"

He leaned close to her. "Child, would you believe? It was Dusty who found you. From what I hear, he was in a van just ahead. He saw the truck go out of control and crash over the embankment. He came back to help. He sent the van driver on for the police while he got you out of the truck and performed CPR. He may have saved your life—that is, Dusty and your seat belt. And the Lord, of course!"

"Dusty rescued me?" she echoed in amazement. "I can't believe it! Where is he?"

"Just outside the door. Chomping at the bit to get in here."

Kasey brushed the tears from her eyes. "Well, send him in!"

"OK, Kasey, but Doc says not to tire yourself. You've been through a lot, and you need your rest." Gramps stood up and opened the door. "Come on in, son. She's as eager to see you as you are to see her. But keep it brief."

Dusty ambled in as Gramps slipped out. "Hi, Kasey," he said softly, sitting down. His hair was combed now, and he had on a dry shirt, but his eyes looked troubled. "You OK?"

She nodded. "Now I am. I thought I'd never see you again."

"Yeah, me too. I thought you were a goner. When I saw you in that truck wrapped around that tree—well, for the first time in my life I prayed to God. And I—I guess He heard me."

She managed a smile. "I was praying for you too. Praying I'd find you, so I could tell you how wrong I was."

"Wrong?"

"Wrong to doubt you. I know you didn't take the money, and I—"

He put his finger to her lips. "Shh. Let's not talk about it now, Kasey. I know about Diana and the whole crazy mess. It's OK. I'll deal with it."

"Then you're not angry with me?"

He moved closer and ran his finger over her nose and chin. "Angry? How could I be angry with you? I'm grateful."

"What for?"

He grinned. "You came after me. You cared enough about me to risk your life to bring me home. No one's ever done anything like that for me before."

"Yes, Someone has," she murmured.

"Naw," he scoffed. "I'da known about it."

"But it's true."

"Who?"

"Jesus. He loved you enough to give up His life to bring you home. Home to Him. I was afraid I wouldn't get to tell you."

141

"You've told me before, in many different ways."

"But you haven't believed it yet, or it would make a difference in your life."

Dusty shrugged. "It's not that I don't believe, Kasey. It's just that I've always had a hard time trusting anybody, even God."

"I know, " she said urgently. "That's why He sent me to you. So if you found someone you could trust—like me—you'd know you could trust God too."

He leaned over and brushed a kiss on her cheek. "God just did me a whopping big favor, letting you be OK. I guess I owe Him one."

Kasey smiled. "We both owe Him *everything*, Dusty."

"OK, so, tell you what. Maybe I'll get to know Him. I'll tag along with you and your grandparents to church on Sundays, if that'll make you happy."

"Absolutely! It'll make me happy, and Jesus too."

He chuckled. "Then it looks like I win all the way around."

"Does that mean you're staying on at the farm and helping out?"

"Right. If your grandparents will still have me."

"Oh, they will!"

Dusty stood up and smoothed his Levi's. "I'd better go and let you get some sleep, kiddo. Besides, your folks will be here any time, and you'll wanna visit with them."

"Dusty, wait. Will you come back?"

He took Kasey's hand and pressed it against his cheek. "Sure, I'll be back. Try and stop me. We're friends, aren't we?"

She felt a smile beam from one side of her face to the other. For sure. Friends forever. Silently she promised, *And one day Jesus will be your forever Friend too!*

Dusty lingered in the doorway, tall, sun-bronzed, and ruggedly handsome. His troubled gaze had given way to eyes filled with tenderness and hope. Gently he whispered, "I'm glad you're OK, Kasey. Good night, special angel. Sleep well."

Kasey smiled dreamily. As she closed her eyes and sank back against her pillow, she knew she would sleep the sleep of the angels.